PRAISE FOR *VICIOUS IS MY MIDDLE NAME*

"Sydney is only a middle school student but she teaches her whole town a valuable lesson in the power of friendship, DIY, and tenacity. This book reminds us that punk is more than just good music and that one great show can change everything."

—Alice Bag, lead singer of The Bags and author of *Violence Girl*

"*Vicious is My Middle Name* is a compulsively readable novel with vivid storytelling and so much heart. It is impossible not to root for Sydney, even as she reveals her flaws and struggles to grow and become a better person. This is a powerful story about learning to be yourself and coping with change. It is a must-read for anyone who has ever felt like a misfit and found solace in books and music."

—Jennifer Whiteford, author of *Grrrl*

"Sydney is funny, fierce, and fearless. She channels a punk rock attitude and do-it-yourself work ethic not only to cope with the daily horrors of middle school, but also to fight to save her community from the dangers of an asphalt plant. Sydney is a hero and a role model for all young people today, taking a stand and hoping to change the world. She definitely would not be holding anyone's coat."

—Nancy Barile, author of *I'm Not Holding Your Coat*

"When a punk grrrl relocates from New York to rural North Carolina, she misses her friends, her music, and more. And then there are the mean girls [kids] to survive. The school power structure is also reflected in the town, however, and battle lines drawn on the first page will widen to put others at risk. But Sydney Vicious Talcott will find allies in unexpected places, a mission bigger than her problems, and will come to see that mountain folk have a punk attitude all their own! An energetic and absorbing read."

—Valerie Nieman, author of *To the Bones*

"In *Vicious is My Middle Name*, Sydney 'Vicious' Talcott is a girl to be reckoned with. When she moves from Rochester, NY to Beaver Dam, NC, she realizes the full meaning of Grrl Power as she takes on the company H.D. Dunkirk and the powers that be when they attempt to construct an asphalt plant close to her school. In her punk rock way, Sydney proves her fierce individual freedom in keeping true to herself and the 'big picture of life.' Kevin Dunn writes in beautiful, hard, measured prose that stays with us long after the last page."

—Mary Sullivan, author of *High* and *Dear Blue Sky*

"Sydney Vicious Talcott's life is disrupted when her mom moves them from Rochester, New York to the small town of Beaver Dam, North Carolina. Readers will root for her as she encounters a bully, an unsympathetic teacher and an environmentally hazardous project backed by powerful and threatening community leaders. Her love of music and determination to take a stand and make a difference propels the reader through this timely story. *Vicious is My Middle Name* is written with skill and a perfect sense of timing, placement and character."

—Roxanne Doty, author of *Out Stealing Water*

"Kevin Dunn is a firm believer in the power of youth, and individuals banding together to improve their community. *Vicious Is My Middle Name* combines these two tenets in an accessible yet fierce paean to punk rock and the way that seemingly small actions can resonate far beyond intention."

—Michael T. Fournier, author of *Swing State*

VICIOUS IS MY MIDDLE NAME

Kevin Dunn

Fitzroy Books

Published by Fitzroy Books
An imprint of
Regal House Publishing, LLC
Raleigh, NC 27587
All rights reserved

https://fitzroybooks.com

Printed in the United States of America

ISBN -13 (paperback): 9781646032808
ISBN -13 (epub): 9781646032815
Library of Congress Control Number: 2021949162

All efforts were made to determine the copyright holders and obtain their permissions in any circumstance where copyrighted material was used. The publisher apologizes if any errors were made during this process, or if any omissions occurred. If noted, please contact the publisher and all efforts will be made to incorporate permissions in future editions.

Interior by Lafayette & Greene
Cover images © by C. B. Royal
Illustrations © by Amanda Kirk

Regal House Publishing, LLC
https://regalhousepublishing.com

The following is a work of fiction created by the author. All names, individuals, characters, places, items, brands, events, etc. were either the product of the author or were used fictitiously. Any name, place, event, person, brand, or item, current or past, is entirely coincidental.

Printed in the United States of America

To Strummer

1

Yankee Go Home!"
    The sign was written in block letters with a black magic marker and taped to my locker. Clearly things were bad, but even then I had no idea how ugly it would get in the coming months.

Trouble had started that morning when the teacher introduced me to the eighth-grade class.

"I'd like y'all to give a big Beaver Dam welcome to our new student from Rochester, New York, Miss Vicious Talcott."

A wave of high-pitched laughter swept through the classroom. I sighed. "Actually, my name is Sydney. Sydney Talcott. Vicious is my middle name."

"Oh yes, I see," she said, looking at the paper in her hand. "Well, welcome to our social studies class. Please take a seat."

I wanted to turn around and walk back out of the classroom. Instead, spying an empty desk at the back of the room, I headed down the aisle. As I moved past the students staring at me, I noticed a small group of kids sitting together, still laughing. They were all dressed almost exactly alike, wearing expensive boots, what looked like the same brand of blue jeans, and red "Beaver Dam Beavers" sweatshirts for the girls, hoodies for the boys.

Hufflepuffs, I thought to myself.

But as I passed, the girl in the middle of the group looked me up and down with disgust, then locked her piercing green eyes on mine and sneered, "Nice hair, freakshow."

The clump of clones around her burst into a loud chorus of giggles. I hurried to my desk as heat rose from my chest, up my neck, and onto my face. That one is pure Slytherin, I corrected myself.

Feeling self-conscious, I glanced down at what I was wearing: a black Epoxies T-shirt with Roxy Epoxy's face on it. Black jeans with the knees ripped up. Purple Doc Marten boots. It was a look I've rocked for years. Classic Sydney Talcott.

Looking around the room I saw that everyone else was wearing hunting camos, button-down shirts, or designer whatevers. No one was dressed as awesomely as I was.

As for my hair, I have great hair.

It's straight and black, reaching my shoulders with the last two or three inches dyed bright red. And the right side is mostly shaved. Like I said, I've got great hair.

Vicious really is my middle name. My parents had a deal that if they were gonna have kids, Dad would name us. He was way into punk rock when my brother and I were born. My older brother is named Joey Ramone Talcott. Not Joseph. Not Joe. Straight-up Joey. He was named after the lead singer of the Ramones, a New York City band that pretty much invented punk.

As for me, I'm named after the bass player of the Sex Pistols, a British punk band. That guy spelled his name "Sidney," but Mom insisted they spell mine with a Y. Dad always said that if I had been a boy, he'd have named me after the Sex Pistols' lead singer. I would have been Johnny Rotten Talcott.

So yeah, there's that.

I actually like my name. Some friends have tried calling me Syd, but it never stuck. I am more of a Sydney.

But that was back when I had friends. Before Mom made us move to Beaver Dam, North Carolina. Right in the middle of my school year. Not disruptive at all. Thanks, Mom.

Rochester has a lot more going on than Beaver Dam, which seems like total Napville. There isn't a single record shop, bookstore, or cool coffee shop here. Back home we had all of those things, even all-age punk shows in the basement of a church less than a mile's walk from my house.

And a lot more kids who looked like me.

"Sydney? Sydney, can you join us please?" Mrs. Critcher's voice brought me back to reality. Another round of snickering erupted.

"Um, sorry, what? I just zoned out a little." More giggles, which seemed to be the primary way these kids communicated around here.

"We're beginning the chapter on the evolution of the American judicial system and I was wondering if you would mind reading the first paragraph on page eighty-seven, dear."

I pulled out the textbook Mrs. Critcher had handed me earlier, found my place, and began to read aloud. After a few sentences, I saw the green-eyed Slytherin waving her arm in the air.

"Yes, Bethany? What is it?"

The girl sat up a little straighter, tossed her blond hair over her shoulders, waited a second, obviously for effect, and then said in a syrupy voice, "Excuse me, Mrs. Critcher. But could you please ask Vicious Sydney to speak English? I can't understand a word she is sayin'!"

A fresh wave of laughter swept through the class.

Half an hour at my new school and the mean kids were already picking on me.

Perfect.

I was pretty sure Bethany and her Brat Pack put the "Yankee Go Home!" sign on my locker door after lunch. They spent the whole lunch period laughing and pointing while I sat by myself at the end of a long table in the cafeteria. There was a whole knot of them, boys and girls, all looking extra crispy. I couldn't tell if there were six or eight or ten of them at the table. It was hard to tell them apart and they looked interchangeable. I think I counted a couple of them twice.

When I got to my locker and found the sign, I tried to act casual. I pulled it down and stuffed it into my backpack, but I could feel the stares on my back and the barely suppressed giggles from the kids standing around me.

For the 387th time that day, I wished Kris were with me. Like a magical charm, she would have given me strength and support. Best friends since first grade, we shared the same twisted, silly sense of humor. She and I were always playing "Sorting Hat," in which we guessed which Hogwarts' house people would belong to: Gryffindor, Slytherin, Ravenclaw, or Hufflepuff. It's a Harry Potter thing.

We were both Ravenclaws. Naturally.

No one got me like Kris got me.

Plus, we shared the same interest in music and books.

Since I was a kid I was into music, especially by rad women. Everything from Billie Holiday and Ella Fitzgerald to Debbie Harry and Sinead O'Connor. I'd spent my childhood flipping through my dad's massive vinyl collection and if there was a female in the band, I'd wear that album out. I loved the first two Pogues albums with Cait O'Riordan in the band, but couldn't be bothered with their stuff after she left.

Kris and I had been into punk rock since we were eight or nine. Dad had long since moved on to folk and jazz, but Joey was a constant source of punk music and information. He was always turning me on to bands. My bedroom in Rochester was papered over with pictures of famous female punk singers. My huge Roxy Epoxy poster loomed over some smaller magazine cutouts of Kathleen Hanna and Exene Cervenka. I had even printed out pictures of Alice Bag and Dani DeLite and put them into frames.

But that wasn't my bedroom anymore. Mom sold the house at the end of last year.

After I told Kris that Mom and I were moving away, she dyed her short, spiky hair dark blue. To "signify her mourning," she said. "It's called Midnight Blue. I was gonna go with black, but Midnight Blue just sounds way cooler."

We were walking home from school, up her street, like we did most days. Kris was kicking an empty soda can ahead of her on the sidewalk, which she had been doing for the last block. "What's Badger Dam like, anyway?" she asked.

"It's called Beaver Dam, as you well know." We both laughed at the joke she had made a dozen times already. "It's really small and boring. There's a hardware store. I think there might be a flower shop or something like that. A few touristy stores selling cheap crafts. If I'm downtown, I spend my time in the old library."

"Of course you do," Kris said, laughing.

Like I said, Kris got me.

"When we've visited in the past, we've mostly stayed on Granny and Grandpop's farm outside of town. It isn't a big farm or anything, but they've got chickens and gardens with vegetables and flowers. It's super boring. And it's so hilly, skateboarding can be a life-threatening adventure."

I told her the story of the summer when I tried riding my old skateboard down a steep hill. The smooth paved road had suddenly turned into gravel and I totally wiped out. Mom banned me from skating for the rest of the summer.

"I remember that!" Kris laughed. "When you came back, you still had little bits of grit under your skin!" We laughed our way up her driveway and into her house.

Man, I missed Kris.

When the school bell finally rang, I gathered up my backpack from my locker and pushed my way out the front of the building where a handful of buses were waiting. I scanned the buses for number 38, which was sitting at the end of the line. As I walked toward my bus, the freezing cold wind sent a chill down my back and I tightened the scratchy wool scarf around my neck.

"Ravenclaw? Jabber? Minor Threat?" It took me a second to recognize Bethany's voice (the predictable chorus of giggles clued me in) and another second to realize that she was reading the buttons and patches covering my backpack.

For the last year, Kris and I had been making our own buttons with one of Joey's old button-makers. The ones on my backpack were mostly of bands that I liked, plus a few girl-power ones.

"Oooooh, so *that's* what a feminist looks like!" Bethany said, acknowledging one of the bigger pins. "I always knew they would look—and smell—like that."

Look like what? I wondered as I walked faster toward the bus. Climbing aboard, I took the first empty seat I saw. Glancing out the window, I saw Bethany surrounded by a pack of kids. They were clumped together so closely, it looked like a pile-up of expensive winter jackets, starched jeans, and trendy boots. When they got to a massive black SUV in the parking lot, Bethany reached for the front passenger seat while the other four—two boys and two girls—squeezed into the second row of seats. It was one massive suburban assault vehicle.

Nobody sat next to me on the bus, which was just as well. I was usually pretty strong and could put up with a fair amount of teasing. I had an older brother, after all. But I just felt so tired. Anger was being drowned by despair. If anyone spoke to me, especially if they were nice, I feared I might start crying.

From my backpack I pulled out a worn copy of the *Rochester Skate City* zine that I had made last year with Kris and a few other skateboarding girls. It was mostly collages of pictures we had taken, along with short write-ups of our favorite places in Rochester to skate. I started flipping through it, but the photos just reminded me of what I was missing. After a few tears landed on the pages, I put the zine away and stared out the window.

As the bus made its way to Granny and Grandpop's house—I guess it was my "home" now, but I still couldn't think of it that way—I distracted myself with the scenery outside. The bus drove through the town and then out into the countryside. We passed old farmhouses, churches, and thick stretches of forests along the curving road.

I tried to remember all of the landmarks in Rochester that Kris and I would pass on the way home from school. There was a Vietnamese restaurant, a Korean grocery store, and a vegan doughnut shop (so good!) on the last block before the bus would turn onto Kris's street. Thinking about those places, and especially Kris, almost made me start crying again.

When I got off the bus across from Granny and Grandpop's house, I'm sure the tears in my eyes were caused by a blast of cold wind.

I pushed my way inside the kitchen and the warmth from the old wood stove in the corner smacked me in the face like a hot pillow. My nose immediately started to run. I hadn't realized how cold I had gotten from the long walk up their driveway. Their old farmhouse was set back a fair distance from the road in a little holler between the mountains (okay, steep hills). A shallow creek meandered through the back of their property. I'd loved playing in it during summer visits, but I hadn't been back there yet, assuming the stream was iced over. The gardens out back were visible from the big windows of the kitchen.

Granny was standing by the sink, washing out two coffee mugs. "Have a seat, sweetheart. I just put on some hot chocolate and I'm warmin' up some of last night's pumpkin pie. Would you like a slice?"

"That would be great, Granny. Thanks." I dropped my backpack on the floor and sat down at the old wooden kitchen table. The table was stained and pockmarked with dozens of dents and scratches. I peeled off my army jacket and scarf, but kept my thick sweater on, despite the heat coming off the wood stove. "Is Mom here?"

"No. She went over to the university to get her registration sorted out. She shouldn't be back till suppertime."

Granny poured the hot chocolate from a saucepan that had been warming up on the stove. She set one mug down in front of me and sat down across the table with the other one. She was wearing a big flompy sweater and an old frayed apron that I was beginning to suspect she lived in. Granny kept her gray hair pulled back, and her reading glasses were pushed on top of her head. Her wrinkled cheeks were rosy from the heat in the kitchen.

"There you go, sugar. The pie will be ready in just a few minutes. So," she said, looking at me over the rim of her mug as she blew on the hot chocolate, "how did your first day at school go?"

I blew on my own hot chocolate, enjoying the way the steam circled around my face, while I organized my thoughts. I didn't want to start dumping on Granny. I feared that if I started to complain about the homesickness I was feeling, I'd start to cry again. Plus, I didn't have the closest relationship with my grandparents. I mean, I loved them and everything. They'd been nothing but kind to me over the years. But I hadn't spent much time with them. They had never visited us in Rochester, saying that they couldn't leave the farm alone for very long.

"It was okay, I guess." I kept my eyes on the melting marshmallow in my hot chocolate. I felt her eyes trying to read me.

"Mmm-hmmm. Well," she started, but was interrupted by the loud clomping of Grandpop on the side porch. We heard him stomping the icy mud off his boots, then kicking them off before entering the house. Granny was constantly nagging people to take off their boots before they walked into the house. I realized that I hadn't taken my boots off yet, and I started to untie the laces under the table. The fact that she hadn't mentioned it to me must have taken enormous willpower. She was probably giving me a pass because she knew I'd be fragile after my first day of school, and I felt a flood of gratitude and affection for her.

The door swung open and Grandpop padded into the kitchen in his thick wool socks, walking with a slight limp. He was tall and skinny, and his thick, bushy white hair almost scraped the top of the doorframe. Before he retired, he'd been a building inspector for the town of Beaver Dam, but I'd always imagined him as a wizened Hogwarts wizard.

"Afternoon, Sydney. Havin' some hot cocoa?" He spoke with a deep, gentle rumble of a voice.

"Yes, we are," Granny said. "There's some more on the stove. You can have some after you wash those filthy hands. And while you're over there, you can take the pie out of the oven so Sydney can have a slice."

After a minute, Grandpop came to the table with a mug of hot chocolate and three plates of pumpkin pie. He gave me the biggest slice.

"Sydney was just tellin' about her school day. Did you make any new friends, sweetie?"

"Not quite." I laughed, thinking about Bethany and her gaggle of gigglers. I took a bite of the pie. Oh man, it was so good. Granny was the queen of pies.

"Well, that'll come, dear. Just give people time to get to know you. And you to know them. I'm sure you'll make some dear friends." She nibbled a bite of her pie.

I didn't say anything, but thought that I certainly wouldn't meet anyone as cool as Kris. Feeling the tears welling up again, I kept my head down and dug into the pie. Grandpop asked Granny if she wanted anything from the grocery store in town, which sent Granny on a five-minute rant on how expensive food had become since the old Harris Teeter had been replaced by a newer, bigger one out on Laurel Ridge

Road. While she was still in mid-rant, I excused myself, took my dishes to the sink, and went up to my room.

"My room" had been Mom's room when she was growing up. She said she couldn't face moving into her childhood room when we arrived a few weeks before, so she took her sister Kate's old room. I'd taped my poster of Roxy and the photos of Alice, Kathleen, and Dani on the walls when I first moved in, even before I unpacked my clothes. Over the desk was a collage of personal photos, mostly of Kris and me goofing around. I took the crumpled "Yankee Go Home!" sign out of my backpack and taped it next to the pictures. Then I curled up on the bed under a pile of quilts and started to cry.

Mom didn't come home until after dinner, and she spent the whole time talking about her day, the challenges she had getting registered as a continuing student, and her excitement about her classes.

"I was worried I was going to stick out like a sore thumb as the only adult on campus, but there were loads of mature students walking around. And the advisor they assigned me is head of the accounting department, and I'm in two of her courses this semester, so that is a good connection to have. Momma, is there any more soup left?" she asked, scraping the bottom of her bowl.

We'd finished our own supper just as she walked in, but stayed at the kitchen table watching her eat and talk. I was folding and refolding my napkin into different shapes. Grandpop pushed back from the table, taking Mom's bowl over to the stove for a refill. Mom had been talking about herself nonstop since she walked in.

I was fine not talking about my day, but when Mom briefly turned her attention to the new bowl of soup Grandpop had set in front of her, Granny cleared her throat. "I think Sydney had a good first day at school too."

Before I could say anything, Mom continued with her monologue.

"Well, I hope it went smoother than my day went. I tell you, it's a bureaucratic nightmare trying to deal with all the red tape. I sent in my application months ago," she said. Granny caught my eye and smiled at me. I continued to refold the napkin, this time trying to make a swan. I tuned my mom out and wondered what was going on back in Rochester. Was Kris sitting down with her family in their small kitchen? What was Joey doing? Probably standing over the sink eating a toasted bagel, if I knew him.

"Sydney?" Mom's voice brought me back to the cramped kitchen in Beaver Dam. "I was just asking if you made any interesting friends today?"

"I met some interesting people, for sure. But none that I would consider a friend. Or even friendly, for that matter."

"Tomorrow will be better, I'm sure of it. I just hope I can meet some folks my age in my classes. I'm pretty nervous about the statistics course, since I haven't had an advanced math class in decades." And she was off again.

Later that night, back under my pile of quilts, I watched the snow softly falling outside of my window. Was Kris watching snowflakes falling outside her window? Was it snowing on Joey's campus in Buffalo? Was there snow covering Dad's grave?

As sleep slowly crept up on me I wondered if tomorrow would be as bad as today had been.

Probably, I thought to myself.

Probably worse.

2

I was right. The next day was worse.

It started off fine. The bus driver, a grumpy grandfather-looking guy named Mr. Benchley, drove along twisting mountain roads with a beautiful blanket of snow covering everything. I could see the ridges of the mountains stretching out in the distance, like white crested waves frozen in space. Okay, I'll admit that the morning bus ride to school was far nicer in Beaver Dam than it had ever been in Rochester, where the bus drove down city streets covered in dirty snow. One point for Beaver Dam.

The morning classes were uneventful. We were covering almost the same material as I had been studying in Rochester, so I felt like I was on top of it, and in a lot of ways, ahead of the classes. So, two points for Beaver Dam.

The only real challenge came in English class because I got the feeling the teacher, Mr. Snead, didn't like me at all. I had been placed in the advanced literature class. We were reading *Catcher in the Rye*, and I may or may not have rolled my eyes when he told me that.

"Do you have a problem with that, Miss Talcott?" he asked as he handed me a well-worn copy of the book. Someone had drawn a line of stick figures at the bottom of the cover and the back was held together with packaging tape.

"Uh, no. It just…you know…"

"I know *what*, Miss Talcott?" He glared at me.

"Well, it's kind of cliché to assign *Catcher in the Rye*, isn't it? Plus, it's kind of a *dude* book, you know."

"Actually, Salinger isn't typically assigned until high school. But cliché or not, what I do know, Miss Talcott," he said, turning abruptly on his heel and walking back toward his desk in the front of the room, "is that the book is considered a classic and we will be reading it over the next two weeks before we begin our poetry module."

Like I said, I don't think he likes me very much.

Did I mention his sweater vest? So ugly.

But things got much worse at lunchtime. I had brought a bagel with cream cheese for lunch. A few days before, I had been excited to find bagels at the Harris Teeter grocery store (the one Granny hates) because I love bagels so much. But this thing was horrible. It tasted like a stale hamburger bun pressed into the shape of a bagel. Minus five points for Beaver Dam.

I was just thinking that it should be illegal to even call it a "bagel" when Bethany and three girls walked up. Bethany and her blow-dried buttheads were all wearing leggings and sweaters, but at least this time they were different colors.

"Oh, Vicious Sydney," Bethany sneered. "We're startin' a collection to buy you some new clothes since you're wearin' them same ratty jeans from yesterday."

Cue cackling from the clueless choir.

For the record, I was wearing a different, clean pair of jeans. It's just that it, like most of my jeans, had the knees blown out.

The long underwear underneath may have been the same from the day before. I can't swear to that.

"But I'm not sure there is a thang we can do 'bout your head." She pointed to the shaved section and dropping her voice slightly. "Did the razor slip when you were shavin' your moustache?" More giggles from her entourage.

I gave her my best why-were-you-born look. "You're hi-larious. Is that why you have to walk around with your own laugh track?"

Okay, it wasn't my best comeback. I was off my game.

"Uh, hello." Bethany held her hand up to her ear to mimic talking on the phone. "Yeah, one second." She pulled the "phone" away from her ear and covered it with her other hand. She glanced down at my blue-and-black flannel shirt and my Nirvana T-shirt, then stage-whispered to me: "Grunge is callin'. They want their clothes back!"

The three stooges fell out laughing.

Rolling my eyes, I stood up, pushed past them, and walked out of the cafeteria, pausing only to throw my half-eaten "bagel" away. Negative ten points for Beaver Dam.

I wandered down the hallway toward the school library. When Mrs. Critcher had welcomed me to school the day before, she'd mentioned that I could eat lunch in the cafeteria or the outdoor courtyard. Or if I didn't want to eat, I could hang out in the library. Seeing that the cafeteria was infested by Bethany and her Butthead Brigade and that the courtyard was freezing and covered with snow, I headed toward the back of the school where the library addition had been built, almost as an afterthought.

I pushed the library door open a tad bit too hard. It slammed open and the young librarian behind the front desk shot me a look. If you could say "shhhh!" with a glance, she did. Gryffindor, I thought to myself.

"Sorry," I whispered.

I wandered around the library, not looking for anything in particular. Mostly I just wanted to kill time and avoid people. My cheeks still felt a little flushed from my exchange with Bethany and I was worried I might punch someone or start crying if I had to talk to anyone else.

Turning a corner in the bookshelves, I saw a Harry Potter poster on the back wall. It promoted reading ("Unlock the magic of a book!") and had a picture of Hedwig the owl, who is hands-down my favorite character in the whole series. Taking this as a good sign, I walked toward it. Maybe there would be a copy of a Harry Potter book that I could read for the rest of lunch period.

As I got to the back wall, the book stacks opened slightly, exposing a small table where two kids sat, immersed in books. The boy was skinny with dark skin and glasses. The girl was heavier, wearing a bulky sweatshirt with a Deathly Hallows symbol on the front. They both looked up when I came around the corner. The boy jumped a foot out of his chair and dropped the book he was holding.

"Uh, sorry," I said.

The boy let out a high-pitched squeak that sounded like "Don't hurt me!"

I did a double-take. "Excuse me?"

The girl let out a sigh. "C'mon, Shawn."

The boy was shaking in his chair, looking at me.

"What did you say?" I assumed I hadn't heard him correctly. Maybe the accent was confusing me.

The girl sighed again and turned to me. She spoke with a slight Mexican accent. "He thinks you're gonna to beat him up or something."

"That I'm gonna beat him up?" I repeated dumbly. That might have been the craziest thing I had heard all month, which was saying something. "Why would he think that?"

"Well, for one thing, you're the new kid from a big tough northern city, dressed like a gang member."

"A gang member?" I looked down at my clothes.

That'd be one cool gang, I thought to myself.

"For another, Shawn is the biggest wimp in the world. It's pathetic, really."

There was a noise behind me and the librarian came around the corner, looking concerned. Definitely a Gryffindor. "Is everything okay here?" She glanced at me, and then looked over at the other two. "Rita? Shawn?"

"It's fine, Ms. Yancey. Shawn just got surprised and dropped his book."

Coming to his senses, Shawn picked the book up off the floor and then pushed his glasses back up his nose. "Yeah, sorry 'bout the noise, Ms. Yancey." He spoke in a slow drawl.

The librarian, a youngish woman with her dark brown hair pulled pack in a severe ponytail, glanced back at me suspiciously and walked back around the corner. I suspected she wasn't going far.

"Uh. Sorry to surprise you. I was just looking for some-place to hang out."

"The cafeteria not your scene, huh?" The girl moved the backpack off the seat next to her and motioned for me to sit down. "Us too. It's kinda Clique Central in there. Not hospitable for book nerds like us. I'm Rita and this is Shawn. Your name is Sydney, right?"

I sat down in the newly vacated seat. "Yeah, Sydney Tal-cott. Thanks."

I looked at the pile of books on the table between them. "What are you guys reading?"

Shawn held up the book in his hand. "Philip Pulman's *His Dark Materials* trilogy. This is the first book and the other two are right here," he said, pulling two books out of the pile.

"I'm re-reading *Harry Potter and the Goblet of Fire*," Rita said. I'd already pegged her as a Ravenclaw and him as a Hufflepuff.

"Yeah," Shawn scoffed. "For, like, the five hundredth time."

"Well, it *is* my favorite in the series."

"Mine too," I said. "I love all of the Tri-Wizard challeng-es. Plus, I like how J.K. killed Cedric off at the end. It showed she was willing to sacrifice major characters."

Rita brightened considerably. "Exactly!" Turning to Shawn, she said, "See? Sydney understands!"

Shawn shrugged, waving a carrot. "Blah blah blah. *Prison-er of Azkaban* is obviously the best, whatever you two may think."

"Um, do you happen to know which Hogwarts House you are in?" I asked.

"We've done all the online quizzes and for some reason Shawn keeps coming out as Gryffindor." Without looking up, Shawn raised his fist in mock triumph. Rita rolled her eyes at him. "I'm definitely a Ravenclaw."

"Me too!"

Rita smiled. "Of course you are! Who are your favorite characters?"

I was just about to reply when the bell sounded. Shawn and Rita started putting books into their backpacks. I noticed they were also packing up their lunch bags. "I thought we weren't allowed to eat in here. And don't you have to check those books out?"

"Some of these are our own copies," Shawn said. "But Ms. Yancey lets us take books out whenever we want. She's cool about it because she knows we'll bring 'em back in a day or two."

Rita tossed her backpack over her shoulder. "Yeah. And she lets us eat lunch over here where no one can see us. Just as long as we keep everything clean."

She looked at me a little shyly. "You can join us tomorrow, if you want."

"Uh, yeah. That'd be cool." I suddenly realized that I had made friends with two fellow book nerds, even if one was a Gryffindor. I felt a little tingle of excitement.

"Okay, cool. I'll see you later. I think we may have a couple of classes together."

After school let out, I made sure to steer clear of Bethany and her pack of piranha on my way to the bus. I had just sat down in an empty seat and was pulling out my *Rochester Skate City* zine when I heard my name being called. I looked up to see Shawn coming up the aisle.

"Mind if I sit here?"

"Sure."

I picked up the backpack I had put on the seat to

discourage anyone from sitting next to me and dropped it on the floor between my feet.

"So how do you like Beaver Dam so far?" He pushed his black plastic-framed glasses up his nose. He probably needed new, better-fitting glasses. And maybe in a style from the last decade.

"Um, it's okay, I guess. I really haven't had a chance to get to know it well."

"Is it very different from where you're from?"

I laughed. "Uh, yeah! Rochester is a pretty big city. We've got a huge downtown and there are lots of cool neighborhoods with plenty of stores, restaurants, and things to do. And way more people."

"Huh. Doesn't sound appealing to me. No offense, but it sounds like a lot of noise, traffic, and people bumpin' into each other."

"Nah, it's cool. Well, yeah, there can be some traffic sometimes. And the snow does get dirty during the winter, but there is so much going on." I paused, thinking about Kris and our circle of friends. "And there are a lot more people like me, you know."

"Yeah, I get that," Shawn replied. "In case you didn't notice, I'm the only brown face on this bus."

Glancing around, I confirmed that all the other kids were white.

"In fact, I'm the only Black kid in our entire grade," he told me.

"Well, I guess that's another way Rochester is different. My best friend, Kris, is Vietnamese-American." I felt a sharp pang in my heart, just mentioning her.

Now that I thought about it, I realized that I hadn't seen a lot of students of color in my new classes. I glanced out the window as we rolled through the snow-covered town. "Beaver Dam is pretty, uh, snow white," I added, pleased with my joke.

"Oh, it's got color. You just have to look for it."

"Why did your family move here?"

"We didn't. We're from here. I'm Appalachian born and bred. As are my parents and my grandparents and their parents. My kin go back for generations. In fact, we were here before most of these other folks were," he said, gesturing to the other kids on the bus. "I'm a Tucker." He looked at me as if I should know what that meant. I looked back at him blankly. "As in Tucker Mountain? Tucker Hollow? Tucker Creek?"

"Sorry. I got nothing. Is that supposed to mean something?"

"The Tuckers and a bunch of other Black families settled around Beaver Dam before there even was a Beaver Dam. We were here living peacefully with the Cherokee before the Revolutionary War. After the War, whites pushed the Cherokee out. They tried to drive us out too, but we hunkered down around Tucker Mountain, where we've been ever since. We're part of the Black communities in the mountains that my uncle Frank calls Affrilachians."

"Really? I had no idea."

"Most people don't. We get ignored in the history books. Everyone knows bluegrass music, but people forget that the banjo came over from Africa. Like I said, there's lots of color 'round here. You just need to know where to look."

When I got to Granny and Grandpop's house, Granny was in the kitchen making a huge pot of soup. "Shoes!" she called out as I walked in. Dang, I guess my free pass was over.

"Sorry." I unlaced my boots and placed them in front of the wood stove to dry. "Where's Grandpop?"

"He drove into town with your momma. Her car wouldn't start this morning. Somethin' wrong with the battery, I think. Said he was gonna run errands in town until she got finished with her classes. But if this snow picks up"— she glanced out of the kitchen window at the big flakes slowly falling— "they are gonna have a time of it. Do you have any homework, honey?"

"Yeah, a little."

"Well, why don't you get it out of the way 'fore supper? We may have to eat without your mom and Grandpop. It'll be ready 'round six. Oh, and there's a letter there for you," she said, pointing to an envelope on the kitchen table, propped up against the cobalt-blue salt and pepper shakers.

I recognized Kris's handwriting and my heart skipped a beat. Yes!!

I grabbed the letter and headed upstairs. When I got to my room, I dropped the backpack by my desk and jumped onto my bed. Homework could wait. I crawled under the pile of quilts and opened the envelope. It was three pages long!

Kris and I were old-school when it comes to communicating. When we were nine, Kris went to a summer camp where they weren't allowed to use any form of technology for a whole month. So we started writing letters to each other. We would illustrate them with little drawings and include collages that we made from old magazines. It was fun, so we just kept doing that whenever we were apart. It was our thing.

I read her letter once quickly, and then read it again, relishing each sentence. There wasn't much information in it, but it felt like a small portal had opened up, connecting me to back home. She gossiped about goings on in school: two idiot boys fought during lunch; our friend Sasha broke up with her "boyfriend" yet again; our favorite teacher, Mrs. Calabrese, was pregnant and going on leave in April. Kris mentioned going to an all-age show at the Record Archive featuring a couple of cool punk bands and a heavy metal band that she thought was atrocious. Kris was even more judgmental than I was about music. But mostly Kris just talked about how much she missed me and how sad she was with me gone.

I'd been excited when I opened her letter, but now, after reading it twice, I felt the crush of homesickness pressing down on me. All my strength seeped out of my bones, and I curled up in a ball under the quilts.

I must have fallen asleep because I had the craziest dream. Bethany and her high-heeled hellions chased me down a never-ending hallway. At first there were just three of them, and then more and more kids joined in, all looking exactly the same. We started out in the school but then the building transformed into a hospital. I ran into a glass wall at the end of the hall, and on the other side my dad and Joey sat eating breakfast. I slammed my fist on the glass to get their attention, but they kept eating and talking to each other, oblivious to me. I heard a noise behind me and turned around to see that my pursuers had turned into a pack of angry, snarling dogs that were closing in on me.

I awoke with a jolt, feeling even more tired. I hadn't dreamt about my dad in weeks and I lay in bed awhile, feeling shaken and drained.

After dinner, feeling a bit better thanks to Granny's pecan pie, I went back to my room to do my homework. But first I wrote a letter to Kris, telling her about my dream and about ridiculous Bethany and her mindless minions. I didn't mention Rita or Shawn. It just felt wrong telling my best friend in the world about making new friends. Instead, I ranted about how cliché it was that we were reading *Catcher in the Rye* and what a dweeb Mr. Snead was. I ended with a drawing of Kris and me holding skateboards.

It was a pretty good drawing, if I say so myself.

The next day, I spent most of the morning looking forward to lunch. I even ignored another of Bethany's snide comments about my accent in Mrs. Critcher's class.

"Does she have marbles in her mouth or somethin'?"

"That's quite enough, Bethany," Mrs. Critcher said.

Whatever. She was one to talk. As Granny would say, her accent was so thick you could spread butter on it.

When the bell finally rang for lunch, I made my way to the library. I was pretty sure Ms. Yancey gave me a funny look when I said "Hi." Rita and Shawn were already sitting at their table, each with a book in one hand and a partially eaten sandwich in the other. They looked so silly that I couldn't help but laugh.

Shawn jumped a little bit, but not as badly as he had done the day before. Man, that kid was skittish. "Oh, hi, Sydney," he said.

Rita cleared the books off the seat next to her. "Hey, glad you could join us. Do you want to read one of these books? I've got the first four from the Harry Potter series."

"No thanks," I said, sitting down and pulling out my lunch. "I need to read *Catcher in the Rye* for Mr. Snead. Shawn, aren't you in advanced literature as well?"

"Yep," Shawn said, without looking up from his book. I noticed he was now on *The Subtle Knife*, the second book in the *His Dark Materials* trilogy. "I was sittin' two rows over from you yesterday."

"I thought so, but I wasn't sure."

"You were probably too busy trash talking on Salinger to notice." A slight smile danced across his face, but he still didn't look up.

"Yeah, I think I made Mr. Snead angry. He seems to be in love with this book." I held up my battered copy.

"It's not a bad book," Rita said. "I read it last summer, along with a few other classics I felt like I needed to know about."

I was impressed. I would do that sometimes too, getting books out of the Rochester library that Joey had been assigned. "What else did you read?"

"Let's see." She set both her book and her sandwich down so she could count titles off on her fingers. "I started off with some Latino and Latina writers, like Gabriel Garcia Marquez and Isabelle Allende. Then I read George Orwell's *1984*, which was pretty good. *Fahrenheit 451, Little Women, Tom Sawyer*, a little Sherlock Holmes and some Agatha Christie stories, which were really good. And I tried to read *Moby Dick*, but just couldn't get into it."

"I love Agatha Christie. Poirot is the best."

"Me too! But I like the Miss Marple stories better. *4.50 from Paddington* is so good!"

We spent the rest of the lunch period talking about our favorite books. It was amazing how many we both liked. Rita and I talked so much, we didn't even get a chance to read the books that we had with us. Shawn kept reading through our conversation, occasionally expressing his opinion about whatever book we were discussing, without ever looking up from his own book. He excelled at multitasking.

I was legitimately bummed when the bell rang for us to get to class. We grabbed our stuff and headed out of the library, walking past Ms. Yancey at the front desk.

"Aren't you a bit young for that?" she asked, gesturing toward my chest where I held my copy of *Catcher in the Rye*.

"Uh, no," I said, confused. "It's the required reading for Mr. Snead's English class."

"No, not the book. Your Ramones shirt. You seem a bit young to know about them."

I looked down at my T-shirt with the iconic Ramones logo on it. It had been a birthday present from Joey a couple of years before, because he was tired of me always borrowing his.

"My brother gave it to me. He was named after their lead singer. I love the Ramones."

"Me too. I saw them when I was in college. Probably the greatest show I've ever been to."

Holy crudola. Could this be true? Was the school librarian really a Ramones fan?

Suddenly life in Beaver Dam seemed slightly cooler than I had imagined.

3

For the rest of that week, I met Rita and Shawn in the library, where we'd eat our lunch, read, and talk about books. That Friday, Rita wasn't at the table when I arrived, but her bag was in one of the chairs. Soon after I settled in, Rita rounded the corner with a pile of books in her arms.

"Here, take a look at these." She set the books down in front of me. "I think you'd enjoy them, unless you've already read them."

"Wow, thanks." I flipped through the stack, looking at the covers. "I've read this one before. I loved it. Definitely worth reading again," I said, holding up Andrew Weir's *The Martian*.

"The rest may be a little more out there, I think. Some sci-fi, a few historical fiction. That last one is a graphic novel."

I looked at the bottom book and recognized the cover immediately. "Oh, get out! I love *The Lumberjanes*. I own all of the issues and I buy every new one at the Record Archive. Well, I used to buy them there." A pang of homesickness shot through my stomach. I'd never go to the Record Archive to buy another *Lumberjanes* ever again.

"Is that a record store back in Rochester?" Rita looked at me sympathetically.

"Yeah, my best friend Kris and I would skateboard down there every weekend. It's this huge warehouse space that has loads of records and books. There's a little café in the back where they put on all-age shows. It's probably one of my favorite places. Where do you find books and records here?"

"Off the internet mostly," Shawn said.

"There is the college bookstore over in Franklin," Rita added, "but I think they only have textbooks."

"Internet," said Shawn again, from behind his book.

Rita ignored him. "I think there is a used record store in Franklin, but I've never been in. It looks a bit sketchy."

"A sketchy-looking used record store? Sounds like my idea of heaven," I joked.

Rita raised her eyebrows.

Okay, so maybe we didn't have everything in common.

I missed Kris.

Every morning and afternoon I would sit with Shawn on the school bus. Sometimes we'd quietly read our books, but usually he'd point out the window and talk about the places that we were passing, like he was my personal tour guide. Even though we were driving past the same things twice a day, he never repeated himself. It was amazing how much he knew about the mountains. Pointing out peaks with names such as Table Rock, Flat Top, Hawksbill, and Chimney Stacks, he would share stories of folklore. "See that hillside way over there?" He pointed toward a rounded hill covered with a patchwork of pastures and woods. "That's Shady Grove. Some folk claim that it's *the* Shady Grove."

I looked at him blankly.

"You know, Shady Grove? *The* Shady Grove."

"Sorry. I got nothing."

He started singing softly, slightly embarrassed, "'When I was a little bitty boy, I wanted a Barlow knife. And now I want little Shady Grove to say she'll be my wife. Shady Grove, my little love. Shady Grove, I say. Shady Grove, my little love, bound to go away.'"

"Wait. Is Shady Grove a place or a person?" I asked, confused.

Shawn laughed. "Exactly. The singer is talkin' about a girl, but I think over time the name of the place replaced her name in the song. Folks 'round here say that it was a real girl living on that hill back there. I'm not saying it is true or not, but that's the legend. It's a real old song. Doc Watson sang a well-known version of it."

Passing a wooded area with a high chain-link fence, I noticed a big sign next to a padlocked gate, but we were driving too fast for me to read it. "What's that?"

"Oh, that's been empty for years, but I think they got plans to build somethin' on that land soon. But this creek right here?" He pointed to the good-sized stream that was running alongside the road next to us. "They call it Beaver Creek down here, but really it's the continuation of Tucker Creek. It runs off Tucker Mountain, snakes all the way 'round these parts. It's called different names in different parts of the county, but it's Tucker Creek when it begins. Look, see how it turns here and goes behind the school, just past the football field." Pulling into the school, Shawn pointed out how the creek, now slightly wider, was creating a natural boundary between the school and the woods next to it. "It joins the New River, then heads down the mountains and eventually goes out to sea."

"That's pretty cool."

"It *is* cool. The Blue Ridge mountains are some of the oldest in the world. Way older than the Rockies or the Alps."

We walked off the bus, the cold wind smacking us in the face as big white, fluffy snowflakes drifted around us. I looked at the ridgeline in the distance as the shadow of clouds crept across them. They certainly were far prettier than the drab office buildings back in Rochester.

Any rising sense of happiness was crushed in English class. Mr. Snead had us talking about the themes in *Catcher in the Rye*, particularly the struggles with growing up, or what he kept calling "the liminal stage of adolescence."

Whatever.

"Holden is struggling with the transition from childhood to adulthood, and all the universal challenges that such a transition entails." He walked up and down each aisle, acting like a preacher with the book open in his hands. "Not least of which is puberty." A couple of boys started laughing and whispering to each other. "Boys, please grow up. Mr. Greene, do you have something to say?"

"Uh, no, Mr. Snead," replied the big red-headed boy at the back of the classroom. His friends on either side covered their mouths to conceal their laughter.

"I thought not."

I don't know what possessed me, but I raised my hand.

"Yes, Miss Talcott. Do you have something you'd like to share with the class?"

"Well, I'm not sure I buy this whole 'universal' thing you're talking about."

"Excuse me?" Mr. Snead asked.

"Well, he's a spoiled rich white boy, isn't he?" I heard a few nervous giggles from other students. I hadn't said anything funny, so I wondered why they were laughing. "So this isn't really a story about the...lingle-ality of *all* youth, is it?"

"Liminality. The word is *liminality*, Miss Talcott," Mr. Snead said.

Two rows over, Shawn was leaning forward in his seat trying to get my attention. I glanced over. He was slowly shaking his head, his eyes wide with fear. He was mouthing the word *No* over and over.

"It's just that this story is unrelated to what most of the kids I know experience. And if it's supposed to be about puberty, what about a girl's experience with puberty? It's nothing like whatever Holden is going through."

People had giggled when Mr. Snead said *puberty* but complete silence descended on the class when I said it.

Mr. Snead glared down at me, like a bomb waiting to go off.

I had lots of philosophies in my life, most of which I'd gotten from punk rock. One of them I call WWJJD which

stands for What Would Joan Jett Do? Right then, I knew that
Joan Jett would set that bomb off. So I decided to light the
fuse. "So, when you say it has 'universal lessons,' I think that
is, you know, what Holden Caulfield would call 'bullshit.'"

You could have heard a mouse fart. Mr. Snead's face
turned a shade redder. "You will watch your mouth in my
classroom."

"Oh." I looked around, confused. "Sorry...I guess. But
we *are* reading a book with swear words in it. I'm just quoting
the main character. He'd say it was 'bullshit,' wouldn't he?"

And that's how I earned my first trip down to the principal's office, where I received a warning about my supposed
"bad attitude."

Fine, I'll admit that Joan Jett might not always make the
best spiritual guide. But I'm pretty sure Mr. Snead just hates
me.

"Oh lordy, you should have seen Mr. Snead's head explode!"
Shawn told Rita as we sat in our usual spot in the corner of
the library. Shawn had been talking for at least ten minutes,
gleefully going over every detail as if describing his favorite
horror movie. I had never seen him so animated. He hadn't
even bothered to open any of the books piled in front of
him.

Rita sat there with a stunned look on her face, occasionally glancing over at me, giving me a look that seemed to say
Are you out of your mind?

"What's Mr. Snead's deal anyway?" I asked.

"If this place were Hogwarts, Mr. Snead would be Pro-
fessor Snape! He hates to be interrupted. He hates to be
challenged. He hates—"

"He hates me," I said.

Shawn shook his head. "Mr. Snead is strict with everybody."

Rita said, "He doesn't hate Shawn."

"But, yeah," Shawn said, "after you bad-mouthed the book in front of the class, he might really hate you now."

"That's crazy," I protested. "I didn't do anything! Well, nothing but point out a few of the ways that *Catcher in the Rye* is a crappy book."

Shawn reached over to pick out a book from the pile in the middle of the table. "I tried to warn you. I tried to get you to stop. But, no, you just had to run into the lion's den and punch it right on the nose."

Rita shook her head. "I have English with him right after your class. This explains why he was in such a bad mood today. He even gave us a two-page essay assignment."

"Oh yeah, Sydney," Shawn added, "while you were in Principal Fletcher's office, Snead assigned the class a five-page essay discussing Salinger's insights on adolescence. Due on Monday. So thanks for that. And I'm pretty sure everyone else in class now hates you too."

I sank into my seat. Great. I had managed to anger the teacher and annoy the entire class. But it wasn't my fault. Mr. Snead clearly had it in for me.

When I got home that afternoon, I checked the mailbox for a letter from Kris, but it was empty. The house was empty too. There was a note from Granny saying that she had gone to the hated Harris Teeter to stock up on groceries. The weather channel had been predicting increased snowfall over the next few days, and I knew that Granny, always assuming the worst, was probably preparing for a month-long blizzard.

Mom was probably on campus, whether in class, studying in the library, or at work. She had thrown herself into her new life as a student. But she'd also taken a part-time job at the copy center on campus. She was usually asleep when I got the bus in the morning and wouldn't come home until after dinnertime, sometimes even after I'd gone to bed. I wasn't seeing much of her. Which I was kind of okay with.

I was still mad at her for dragging me down here to Beaver Dam. It was her fault I wasn't living in Rochester and going to school with Kris, and it was her fault that I was going to this crappy school where everyone hated me and the teachers had it in for me. And now that we were living in the middle of nowhere, she didn't even care what was going on with me. All she cared about was herself and getting her stupid accounting degree. She was so selfish!

I went up to my room and put some music on. I selected albums by Blondie, Lite Brite, and Jabber to play on shuffle.

Debbie Harry's voice came blasting through a tiny little wireless speaker connected to the MP3 player that I had bought years before with my own money.

I cranked it as loud as I could and climbed into bed under a pile of quilts.

My parents had always been real strict about technology. We weren't allowed phones, only small MP3 players. Growing up, we never had cable TV, only an old screen hooked up to a DVD player that we'd watch movies on. There was one "family" laptop that was in the kitchen that we could occasionally use to look things up for school or to write papers.

Social media was completely restricted. And Mom increased the restrictions even more after Dad was gone, which was fine with me. Everyone at school was always checking their phones, texting each other, and doing whatever they did on social media. I wasn't interested. Kris's parents were pretty much the same way, but she did have her own phone. We mostly used it to listen to music and find out about new bands. Having no access to social media wasn't a big deal, since the main person I'd always communicated with was Kris, and I saw her every day. Well, it wasn't a big deal until I moved away.

Now, we only communicated through handwritten letters. I was thinking about crawling out of bed to write her another letter when I heard Grandpop clomping up the stairs, calling my name. I kicked off the quilts and opened the door.

"Sydney, you up there?"

"Yeah, sorry. I just had some music on."

"Was that what that racket was? I thought someone was torturin' cats up there. I've been callin' you for several minutes. There's a phone call for you. It's Joey."

"Joey!" I squealed and bounded down the stairs, blasting past Grandpop and into the kitchen, where the phone was sitting on the counter.

"Hey, kiddo," Joey said when I picked up. "What took you so long?"

"Oh, I was just in my room under a pile of blankets, listening to music."

"Uh-huh. Sulking, you mean."

"I was *not* sulking. Okay, maybe just a little bit." My spirits lifted just hearing his voice. He asked how things were living with Granny and Grandpop, and he told me of the time he came for a visit with a mohawk and Granny refused to be seen in public with him. We laughed. I could totally see that happening.

When he asked me about school, I started to complain about how the kids and teachers didn't like me. Suddenly I found myself crying.

"I want to come home, Joey. I want to be back in Rochester with you. With all of us. Back to the way things were before." I was ugly-crying now. I wiped my nose on the sleeve of my flannel shirt.

"I know, kiddo. I know," he said softly. "But you are forgetting how crappy things were. Mom and Dad fought constantly. After the accident, Mom cried all the time. It sucked being in that house. Life here in college is so much better than being at home, and I'm pretty sure living with Granny and Grandpop is a lot better than being alone with Mom in Rochester."

"Yeah. That's probably true," I conceded. And in my heart, I knew it was. "But what about me? I miss Kris and all my friends in Rochester. I've got no one here. Everyone hates me."

"Really? *Everyone* at school hates you?" he said mockingly. I laughed. Joey knew me so well. "Okay, poop-face. I do have two friends at school." I told him about Rita and Shawn, how they were book nerds like me, and how we spent our lunchtime reading books in the library. Then I told him what Ms. Yancey said about my Ramones shirt, which made him really happy. When I told him about Bethany, her carbon copies, and our frequent run-ins, Joey started to laugh.

"I'm sorry." He tried to suppress his laughter. "They do sound horrible. But it is just so perfect, your arch-nemesis is a spoiled, rich, mean girl named Bethany. It's too perfect."

"I know! It's like I'm caught in the middle of a bad movie." I was laughing now too. "But my teachers also hate me. Well, one definitely does." I told Joey the story of my encounters with Mr. Snead, and the essay he assigned the entire class as a way to punish me.

"Well, kiddo. You have two options. Write an essay that tells him all the things he wants to hear and get a decent grade. Or, write what you believe and pay the price."

"So my choice is between a brown-noser B or an honest F?"

"Yeah, and I'm pretty sure I know which one you are going to write."

We both laughed until I was crying again. But this time they were happy tears.

I spent much of the weekend working on my essay for Mr. Snead. There wasn't much to do anyway. I had nowhere to go and nobody to hang out with. Mom was on campus all weekend, either studying or working. Plus, a steady snowfall started Saturday afternoon and continued all day Sunday.

By Monday morning, the snow had piled up. I was hoping

that they would cancel school or at least call a snow delay, but they didn't.

Granny fluttered about the kitchen, complaining about how dangerous it was out in the snow and how it was irresponsible to put kids' lives at risk by making them go to school. Grandpop sat silently at the kitchen table, sipping his coffee. Finally, he pushed back and winked at me. "Well, if Sydney is brave enough to face the elements, I might as well face them too." He put on his boots and his big winter coat, and tromped out to the greenhouse.

Taking that as my cue, I got my army coat on and headed to the top of the driveway to wait for the bus. It had stopped snowing, but it was still windy and cold. Thankfully I didn't have to wait long. A big snowplow came rumbling around the curve with the school bus right behind it.

I found my usual seat next to Shawn, who regaled me with stories of historic winter blizzards. About halfway to school, the bus turned onto Laurel Ridge Road, but the snowplow continued on the main road into town. The snow on our unplowed road was thick enough that Mr. Benchley slowed down even more. A few times, he brought the bus to a crawl. I'll say this for Mr. Benchley: he was a better bus driver than some of the ones I'd had back in Rochester.

As we got closer to the school, we passed the fenced-in lot that I had noticed the week before. We were inching through the snow, and I had a clear look at the sign attached to the gate. It stated: "Proposed site: Beaver Dam Asphalt Plant. HD Dunkirk Industries." There was more written below in smaller letters, but it was covered by snow.

An asphalt plant.

That didn't sound cool.

4

It turned out Rita's family was from Guatemala, not Mexico. I felt a little embarrassed about my mistake.

"Don't worry about it. People do it all the time. Guatemala is a small country compared to Mexico, so we're always living in its shadow. At least you got the continent right. One time a kid asked me if I was a Muslim from the Middle East."

"You're kidding me!" Rita looked nothing like my Middle Eastern friends back in Rochester. There were kids in my old school whose families came from Iran, Syria, and Saudi Arabia. I had been good friends with one girl, Nidal, since elementary school.

"Why did your family move to Beaver Dam?" We were in our usual spot in the library. I'd brought some chocolate chip cookies that Granny had made the day before and was sharing them. Shawn was munching one behind his book.

"My dad and uncles had been migrant laborers for years, moving back and forth between Texas, North Carolina, and New York, finding work wherever they could. It was getting more and more violent back home in Guatemala. After one of my cousins was killed, my dad sent for us and the whole family migrated here."

"Oh, man. That's heavy."

"I was just a baby, not even two years old, so I don't remember any of it. I've never been back to Guatemala, so I don't really have a connection to it."

"So you moved here as a baby?"

"No, I spent most of my childhood in and around San Antonio. That's where I went to elementary school. Even though we stayed in San Antonio, we were always moving around. I went to, like, six different schools over five years."

"Holy crudola, that's rough! This is the first time I've been uprooted. You had it way worse than me." I felt a little ashamed to have ever complained about my situation to Rita, given her circumstances. "Did you ever get used to it?"

"Not really. But that's probably why I became such a bookworm. Books were the constant thing in my life when I was growing up. I never developed close friends, because we were always moving."

Shawn cleared his throat in an exaggerated way. As usual, he was reading, eating, and following our conversation closely. Multitasking was one of his superpowers. Rita laughed. "Yes, Shawn, you were my first close friend."

"Lucky for you," he replied.

"We moved to Beaver Dam about three years ago," Rita continued. "It's been the place that I've lived the longest. At least so far."

"Your parents aren't planning on moving again, are they?" An icy feeling crept in my chest from the realization that my new friend might be taken away from me so soon.

"Well, we're never really sure. But my dad's got a good job working on the road crew. He's been driving a plow this week, but in the summer he works on repaving the roads. He likes it so much better than doing agricultural work in the fields. My mom has a job working at Harris Teeter."

"Do you have any brothers or sisters? I'm sorry that I don't even know that."

"It's okay. I've got two older sisters. One is at the community college and the other is over in Franklin at the university."

Shawn spoke from behind his book. "I'm an only child, in case you were wonderin'."

"Obviously!" Rita and I said at the same time, and then laughed.

"What about you? Do you have any sisters or brothers?" asked Rita.

"I've got an older brother, Joey, who goes to college in

Buffalo. He's gonna major in music composition or something like that. He is crazy talented."

"What about you, do you play any instruments?"

"No, my dad was always trying to teach me stuff on various instruments, but I could never learn. I gave up trying after he was killed."

At the mention of my dad's death, Rita leaned forward and Shawn even put his book down.

"Oh my god, Sydney." Rita said softly. "I had no idea. I am so sorry."

"Thanks," I said. "It was about two years ago."

Two years, two months, and five days, to be exact, I thought to myself.

"He was a musician. Well, an aspiring musician. Mom was always on him about never being successful or being able to hold down a real job. He gave lessons at a local music shop. Guitar, bass, keyboard, piano. You name it, he could teach it. If he didn't know how to play an instrument, he'd teach himself in a week. He was brilliant like that. Unfortunately, the musical genius gene skipped right over me. Dad tried for years, hoping to unlock some secret potential if he just found my 'true instrument.' But he never did."

Rita and Shawn were staring intently, not saying a word. I hadn't talked about my dad in months. It felt both good to share but also painful to think about Dad.

Rita reached across the table and took my hand. "Sydney, I am so sorry. I can't imagine how terrible it must have been for you."

"Yeah, it was rough. I...I..." My voice was quivering. The words just wouldn't come out. I thought I might be able to talk about Dad some more, but I couldn't.

After a few moments of strained silence, Rita asked softly, "Is that why you moved to Beaver Dam?"

I nodded.

"Mom had been in a dark place after Dad died. I mean,

really dark. But a few days after Joey left for college, Mom informed me that we were moving and that she was going back to school as well. There was no discussion, she just dropped that bomb on me. I think she always resented not finishing school and getting her accounting degree. She had been a student at the University of North Carolina and dropped out after meeting my dad when he was on tour with one of his bands. After Dad died, I think Granny and Grandpop offered to take us in if she wanted to enroll at the university over in Franklin. She waited until Joey finished high school before she decided to uproot us. I, uh, didn't take the news too well. I couldn't understand why she was pulling me out of my life in Rochester. I may have thrown a glass or two across the room. I can't remember. It's kind of a blur."

Shawn and Rita sat quietly as I recounted the story. When I finished, Rita said, "I don't know how it feels to lose a parent, but I know being forced to move is really hard. I am sorry you had to go through that."

"You know, even then I totally understood why she wanted to leave. The memory of Dad was just too strong, not just in our house but in the city as well. She would say that she felt his absence everywhere we went." The memory of that crushing grief rekindled some of the pain in my heart. My voice quivered again. "I knew what she meant, because I felt it every day too."

Rita came around the table and wrapped her arms around me. I felt Shawn's hand on my shoulder. Nobody said anything. We just stayed like that until the bell rang.

A few days later, I got my *Catcher in the Rye* paper back from Mr. Snead. As Joey had suspected, I'd written an essay arguing why I thought the book gave a pretty lame view of the "liminality of adolescence."

I'd had to look up *liminality*. It is from a Latin word that means *threshold* and is the feeling of ambiguity and disorientation that occurs during a transition period.

You're welcome.

I wrote how Holden was a pretentious spoiled brat who spent all of his time whining about his privilege. I argued that his experiences as a rich white boy had little to do with my life as a teenage girl from Rochester. I thought I was extremely eloquent in my criticism of the book.

Mr. Snead did not. He gave me a D.

"Ouch, that's pretty harsh," Rita said when we were at lunch.

"Yeah, check out his final comment: 'Ms. Talcott, are you not substituting your own positionality in your critique of Caulfield, thus replicating the failures you ascribe to Salinger'" I read from the bottom of the paper. "I don't even know what the heck that means."

Shawn spoke up from behind his book. "It means you're usin' your own experience as a white working-class female as the accepted norm by which to criticize Salinger for doin' the same thing."

I looked at him blankly. Shawn sighed.

"He's callin' you a hypocrite," Shawn clarified before turning back to his book.

"I am not being a hypocrite. Snead just hates me."

I sat back in my chair, trying to express a sense of hurt outrage. Shawn didn't seem to be buying it.

"What about you? What did you get on the essay?"

Rita chipped in, "Oh, Shawn got a perfect grade from Mr. Snead, no doubt."

"If you must know, I got an A," Shawn replied, without looking up.

"What? That's bogus." This time I was truly outraged. "That's just typical for the patriarchy!"

"Yes, we young Black men really have it easy in this country. Especially 'round these parts."

I sat there for a minute trying to think of a suitable come-back, but I had nothing. My anger slowly faded. Who was I kidding? I had known Snead was gonna pound me for that essay.

"Okay, point taken. But what did you say in your essay?" I asked.

Shawn fished around his backpack and pulled out his own essay. "You're welcome to read it. I know you think the book is pretty awful, but there're some important things about *Catcher in the Rye* that are worth praisin'. For instance, it was cool to have a book told from a teenager's point of view." I began to argue, but he cut me off. "True, it's from a limited point of view, but Salinger opened the door for other writers to follow. That fact alone is noteworthy. Also, Salinger's stream-of-consciousness writing style shows the turmoil and contradictions within Caulfield. I think that's pretty import-ant as well."

Shawn slid his essay over to me, then went back to read-ing his book. The essay was over eight pages long, almost twice the assigned length. I started to read it. Holy cats, was it good. Really good. Shawn was using words I vaguely knew and definitely couldn't spell. Where Mr. Snead had marked up my paper for all the spelling and grammar errors, there were no such marks on Shawn's paper. Instead, Mr. Snead had occasionally written *Good point!* in the margins. By the time I finished, I was humbled by how inferior my essay was. I also felt like I understood *Catcher in the Rye* much better.

When I looked up from reading the essay, Rita was look-ing at me with a knowing smile on her face. I widened my eyes and she nodded. I glanced over at Shawn, who was back behind his book but probably listening to hear anything we might say.

I mouthed to Rita: *He's a genius!*

I know! she mouthed back.

The highlight of every day was definitely lunch in the library with Rita and Shawn. I was doing better than okay in all my classes, except for Mr. Snead's English class. But we've already established that he just hated me for no good reason.

Almost every day, Bethany and her crispy clique took it upon themselves to annoy me. Most of the time they just made fun of the way I dressed or talked. Occasionally Bethany would say something that got under my skin, but most of the time it was pretty lame and easy to ignore.

I rarely saw Mom. She stayed on campus late into the evening. Her assignments were starting to pile up, and she was also spending time at her part-time job in the university's copy shop. Many nights she didn't even get home until after I had gone to bed. Granny and Grandpop basically filled in as parents, which was fine with me.

Joey had been right: Mom had been so depressed after Dad was killed. Sometimes she never got out of bed. If she did, she'd sit in her bathrobe at the kitchen table, drinking coffee and staring out the window. It was almost as if we had lost both parents.

Joey tried to call once a week to check on me, which was sweet. He seemed to be having a great time in Buffalo and was booking punk shows at a venue on campus.

Kris and I got into a routine of writing about two letters each week. It was awesome to come home and see an envelope with her handwriting on it waiting on the kitchen table.

Bus rides weren't as bad as I had feared, since I got to sit next to Shawn and learn from his encyclopedic knowledge of the Beaver Dam area. If Grandpop had driven me directly to school, it would have taken about ten minutes to get there. The bus trip took more than thirty minutes with all the stops and detours down side roads. That was fine by me. Shawn was great company and the views were spectacular. Snow was still covering the ground as January rolled into February.

Even though we were months away from springtime,

Granny and Grandpop both spoke of it frequently and reverently. Well, Granny mostly spoke wistfully of how beautiful the mountains would be once the cold weather let up. When Grandpop talked about springtime, it was usually about what needed planting and when.

Every day on the bus, I would watch the woods and the mountains sliding by the window, often with wisps of fog curling through the branches. I was used to the barren city streets of Rochester, but here, there were so many trees. One morning Shawn tried to explain the difference between the mountain laurels and rhododendron bushes we passed. I was appreciating Shawn's love of the landscape, but I was also paying more attention to the proposed asphalt plant near the school. It was the only part of the drive in which we passed a tall chain-link fence. After so much beauty, it was jarring to see something so ugly. I realized I didn't know much about asphalt plants. I never thought about where asphalt came from or how it was made.

"Shawn, do you know anything about asphalt?" I asked him one morning as we drove past the towering chain-link fence.

"I know it is incredibly sticky. Rita says her dad can never get it off his clothes and boots."

"Her dad?"

"Yeah, her dad works road construction, remember?"

"Oh yeah. Is that what they use asphalt for?"

"Mostly. They heat it up and pave the roads with it."

The bus pulled up in front of the school. We grabbed our backpacks and headed off the bus. "Is it dangerous?"

"What, the asphalt? I guess it could burn you when it's real hot. I think the fumes might be toxic. Maybe? I don't know. You can do some research on it if you want."

"You think there are books on asphalt in the library?" I joked.

"Probably." He looked at me straight-faced. "Plus, there

are things called computers that you can look stuff up on."

"Well, I don't have a computer."

Back in Rochester, the school had given every student their own tablet during the school year. But here in Beaver Dam, they only let you use tablets in specific classes and you couldn't take them home. It felt weird having such limited computer access. Minus five points for Beaver Dam.

"There are several in the library. And Ms. Yancey can help you look stuff up." He added, almost dreamily, "That's her job, and she's very good at it."

It suddenly struck me that Shawn might have a crush on Ms. Yancey. That would make sense. What more could he want from someone than an endless supply of books?

When I got to the library for lunch, my thoughts were still on the asphalt plant. Building something like that right next to a school just didn't seem right.

After dropping my stuff off at the table with Rita and Shawn, I walked up to Ms. Yancey's desk. She wasn't there, so I went searching and found her shelving books in the graphic novel section.

"Excuse me, Ms. Yancey?"

She was so lost in thought, she jumped slightly. Then I realized that she had earbuds in and was listening to music. She quickly popped them out.

"Sorry. Did you need something, Sydney?" I had never told her my name. It made me feel pretty good to find out that she knew it already.

"Yeah. I am interested in finding out about asphalt. I was wondering if you could help me."

"Sure. We can check the catalog." She set down the stack of books she had been holding. Judging from the size of the pile of books she had to shelve, I guessed that the graphic novel section might have been the most popular part of the library. "Is this for a science project?"

"Uh, no. I'm just interested in, you know, asphalt."

She shot me a sideways glance. "Really? You've got a longing to know more about the exciting world of asphalt?"

I laughed. Turned out Ms. Yancey had a sense of humor. I could see why Shawn had a crush on her. Wait, maybe I was developing a crush on her!

"Well, to be honest, I keep seeing that sign for the proposed asphalt plant near the school and I thought I'd learn more about it."

Ms. Yancey stopped and turned to look at me closely. She had suddenly become serious. "Why, exactly?"

I felt a little awkward. Had I said something wrong? "Well, it just seems weird to be building a plant like that right next to a school. I wanted to see if there were any dangers associated with it."

She studied me for a few seconds. It seemed like she was trying to make her mind up about something, but I had no idea what. After another few moments she seemed to have committed to a decision, turned, and continued walking to the computers.

"Here, use this one. But let's not use the catalog. I suspect you'll find more by doing some online research." She typed in a few passwords until she got to a main screen. "I've logged you in to my account, so you can go anywhere on the internet and into any archives you may need to check out." She stood up and let me sit down in front of the computer. "Let me know if you have any problems," she said before walking back toward the graphic novels.

I spent the rest of the lunch period doing research. It turns out asphalt is about as boring as you might have guessed. I read about the history of asphalt and its primary purposes (paving roads was by far its main use). It can be found in natural deposits or it can be man-made. The largest natural source is a huge oil and sand pit in Canada that is bigger than the entire country of England. That's crazy.

I was surprised to find the economics of asphalt kind of interesting. When it was first being used, oil refineries would just give it away for free. But by the end of the twentieth century, companies were getting rich by making asphalt. During the first decade of the twenty-first century, the price of an average ton of asphalt increased by 500 percent. That seemed insane. It turns out that making asphalt could be pretty lucrative. Who knew?

I was just starting to read about the environmental and health costs when the bell rang. But the things I saw definitely freaked me out. I decided that I'd have to do more research tomorrow.

On the way to the bus after school, a snowball whacked me on the back of my head. I turned around to see Bethany standing there, trying to act innocent while several of her funkless flunkies giggled madly behind her.

"Very funny, Bethany. Very mature." My anger rose as the ice descended down the back of shirt. The back of my head stung from the impact.

"What? I didn't do anything, Vicious Sydney. I definitely didn't throw a snowball at that big ol' head of yours," she said, her voice dripping with fake innocence.

I started walking back toward her and her pack of preppies. "Sure you didn't," I said. "But if it wasn't you, it was one of your interchangeable idiots. But I doubt they're capable of doing anything on their own." The giggling stopped as they worked out that I'd just insulted them.

"That head of yours is so humongous it must generate its own gravity field," Bethany continued. "Snowballs must be flyin' into it all the time. To say nothin' about birds, planes, and small meteorites."

"Be careful what you start, Bethany. The last time someone threw a snowball at me, they spent an hour picking up their teeth," I said, in as threatening a tone as I could. The wet ice running down my back and into my underwear was making me really angry.

I took a step closer, but suddenly someone grabbed my arm and pulled me backward. It was Shawn.

"C'mon, Sydney. The bus is about to leave. Don't do anything stupid."

I turned and we walked hurriedly toward the bus. As we got closer, a snowball whizzed past my head, and I heard Bethany yell, "Loser!"

As I walked up the steps of the bus, I turned and gave her the one-finger salute. The bus door slammed shut just as another snowball careened into it.

I turned to see Mr. Benchley, the bus driver, staring at me. I felt embarrassed for a second. But as he put the bus into reverse, I'm pretty sure he was trying to suppress a smile.

When I got back home, an envelope was propped up on the kitchen table for me. The last letter from Kris had arrived a whole week before, and I had wondered why it was taking her so long to write. But as I picked up the letter, I realized it wasn't from Kris. The handwriting was different.

Taking off my jacket and boots (Granny had broken me and now I always took them off as soon as I walked into the house), I flopped down in the big green chair next to woodstove. It was the most coveted seat in the house since it was also the warmest. Granny sat in it every morning doing her crossword puzzles, but when she wasn't around I would usually curl up in it. It was a great place to do my homework, which I pulled out of my backpack. But I needed to read this letter first.

The return address was from a "D. Deluca" in Chicago.

I didn't know anyone in Chicago. I double-checked to make sure it was addressed to me. It was. I ripped open the envelope and took out a one-page letter written in swooping handwriting.

And I about pooped myself.

Dear Sydney!

Hey!! This is Dani from Lite Brite. Your brother Joey gave me your address, so I thought I'd write you a letter. He said you were a big fan, which is super awesome. Thanks so much for the support. Lite Brite played at the U of Buffalo last week for a show that your brother booked. It was really fun. It was a small crowd, but full of fun, beautiful people, which is what it is all about. Joey kept talking about how much you would have loved being there. Sorry you couldn't! He said your mom and you had moved down to North Carolina. He also said you were having a hard time adjusting. I can totally relate! When I was in high school, we had to move. We were living in Los Angeles, where I grew up. LA was awesome. Great friends and sunshine all the time! But my parents got divorced and my mom took me and my sister back to Chicago, where she was from. Man, it sucked! All that snow and cold wind!! And I didn't know anybody. And let's just say the new high school in Chicago was a lot rougher than my old one back in LA had been. I think I spent the first six months crying in my bedroom every day! I don't know if you are feeling that way down in Beaver Dam, but if you are, I TOTALLY get it. But by the end of that first year, I started making some great friends. That is where I met Megan, the guitarist in Lite Brite. She turned me on to punk rock and taught me how to play bass. There were a bunch of other cool friends I made. I had planned on going back to California for college, but I decided to go to school in Chicago because it was so cool. The music scene is so great here. The guys from The Arrivals (do you know them? They are AWE-SOME!) were so supportive when we started Lite Brite. Even though I'm still a West Coast grrrl in my heart, now I can't imagine living anywhere else. So, yeah, if you are feeling lost and lonely in a new place, I think I know what you are feeling. Not that your feelings aren't your own! Just that I empathize. Things got WAY better for me, and I hope they get better for you. Joey said that you are a pretty amazing grrrl, which must be true. If you are thirteen and a Lite Brite fan, you must be super awesome! Anyway, write back if you want to. Your brother says that you write great letters! I love that you write letters instead of emailing. I love to write letters too!! I'd love to hear about you and how you are doing. xoxo DANI

She's used a little heart over the "I" in her name and had drawn a little self-portrait at the bottom of the page with a speech bubble that said "Sydney is a Rock Star!"

Oh. My. Gawd.

Dani from Lite Brite had written me a personal letter! Eeeee!!!

I re-read the letter over and over again. I was bouncing in the chair with excitement. This was so cool.

I ran up to my room to write her back. I ripped up the first
two attempts because I thought I was being too gushy. You
try writing one of your sheroes and you'll see what I mean.
I wanted to play it cool, but it was hard. In the end, this is
what I wrote.

Dear Dani:
Ohmigod, thank you so much for your letter! Yes, I am
your biggest fan!! I have a picture of you on my wall,
along with Exene, Sinead, and other kick-butt women.
That is so cool that you played in Buffalo. I wish I had
been there!! Joey is so lucky. But I'm glad he had the
good sense to book Lite Brite to play. He's a pretty good
brother (but don't tell him I said that!). Thanks for sharing your story about moving to Chicago. And I'm sorry
to hear about your parents' divorce. That must have been
hard. I am glad Chicago is so cool. I do know The Arrivals (Joey loves them!) and also Alkaline Trio, who are also
from Chicago I think. I really miss Rochester. There was
so much to do there! But Beaver Dam is very pretty, especially when it is covered with snow. The mountains are
really gorgeous. And there are so many trees here! I've
made a friend named Shawn who is from here and he is
teaching me a lot about the history of Beaver Dam. He
is Black and proudly Affrilachian (which is what he calls
the Black people who have been here for a long time). I
have another friend named Rita whose family is originally
from Guatemala. I guess we're a little group of outcasts
here. They aren't into punk rock, but they are book nerds
like me. Nobody is into punk around here. It's not like
in Rochester. It's pretty boring, actually. There is a pack
of mean kids that pick on me sometimes, but whatever.
They're losers. Anyway, thanks for the letter. When is the
next Lite Brite album coming out? Are you on tour right
now? Any plans to play in Beaver Dam? Ha ha ha ha!
OK, I should do my homework now. My English teacher

hates me. What were your favorite subjects in school? OK, bye!!

xoxo SYDNEY

But instead of doing my homework, I wrote another letter. This one to Kris. She was gonna be SO jealous!

The next day at lunch, I told Rita and Shawn about my letter from Dani. But they didn't seem to understand how awesome it was.

"That seems cool," was all Shawn said from behind his book.

"It *is* cool! Lite Brite is an amazing band!"

"Would I have heard them on the radio?" Rita said.

"Uh, no. Bands like that don't get played on the radio."

"Why not?"

"That's just not how it works. The songs that get played on the radio are big-name bands on big corporate record labels. Bands like Lite Brite put out their own records or get released by small independent record labels."

"Why don't they get on bigger labels? Aren't they good enough?"

"Of course they're good enough!" I said. "But that's not the point."

"Why not? Don't they want more people to hear their music and buy their records?" Rita looked confused.

"See, that's the whole problem! They make the music they want to make, not to sell a lot of records." This was something Kris and I talked about all the time. Why couldn't Rita understand?

"But if the music they are making is good, then more people would buy it, right?"

"But that's not how it works. Don't be stupid," I said, exasperated.

"I'm not being stupid. I just don't see what the big deal is."

"But it *is* a big deal! People don't decide what gets played on the radio, the big corporations do. Popular music is only popular because it is being manufactured and marketed to the masses. Most of those bands don't even write their own songs. Bands like Lite Brite write their own music, book their own shows, release their own music. That's what punk rock is all about."

"Okay. Whatever. It's not that important." Rita picked up a book to signal that she was finished with the conversation.

Getting up from the table, I snapped, "It is important. Kris would understand how important this is."

Rita acted like she hadn't heard me.

I walked around the library, trying to cool off. I don't know why I was so mad. I'd had conversations like this countless times with people back in Rochester. But usually I had other people on my side, whether it was Kris, Joey, and, once upon a time, Dad.

Dad had been passionate about keeping music independent and free of what he called "corporate control." I didn't understand what he was raging about at the time. But later, listening to punk music taught me that he was right.

I guess I was frustrated that my new friends didn't see that this was something I cared about. Not only did they not get it, but they didn't seem to understand why it was so important. Important to me, but also important in the big picture of life. It was about being authentic to yourself and not being a passive cog in a massive money-making machine.

As I turned the corner in the library, I almost ran into Ms. Yancey, who had her earbuds in and was shelving books. Seeing me, she took out her earbuds. "Did you need to do some more research on asphalt, Sydney?"

I almost said no, but then thought better of it. I had only gotten going the day before. "Uh, yeah. But I can use my own account to log on. It's not a big deal."

"If you don't mind, I'd prefer you use my account if you are going to be doing that kind of research." She said it in a way that seemed odd, as if researching asphalt was some super-secretive activity.

She walked over to the computer table with me and logged in. She paused for a second before heading back. "Let me know if you find anything interesting, okay?"

"Uh, sure."

I spent the rest of lunch period reading about the health and environmental costs of asphalt production. It turns out that prolonged exposure to asphalt, especially the fumes, was really bad for you. They were toxic and caused cancer. I looked out the window at the fog that was clinging to the hillsides around the school. It was often foggy in the mountains. If asphalt fumes were caught up in the fog, that seemed like a bad thing. And there were lots of reports about the environmental damage that asphalt production could cause, especially to nearby rivers and waterways. I thought of Beaver Creek that ran behind the school and throughout the county, all the way down to the Atlantic Ocean.

Ms. Yancey walked by and mentioned that the lunch bell was about to ring. "Did you find anything useful?"

"Yeah. This stuff can be dangerous." I told her what I had found out. "I need to read more about it. This asphalt plant could be bad news."

The bell rang, signaling the end of lunch period, and I headed to the back of the library to gather my things. When I got to the table, Shawn was packing up his bag but Rita was gone.

"Did Rita already take off?"

"She left a while ago."

He hoisted his over-stuffed backpack to his shoulder and pushed up his glasses.

I felt a little guilty for having been rude but just grabbed my stuff and headed out the door.

As I was leaving the library, Ms. Yancey gave me a know-ing look. "See you on Monday, Sydney?" It seemed more of a question than a statement.

"Yeah, see you Monday."

On the bus ride home, Shawn and I discussed our plans for the poetry appreciation assignment that was due the follow-ing week for Mr. Snead.

Mr. Snead had explained that he was giving us a "range of tools that we could use for analyzing and appreciating any poem." In each class we had worked on learning a new tool, or step. He was pretty pompous about it, if you ask me.

"If we develop our toolbox of analytical tools, we can better understand how poetry works and why," he'd explained on the first day. "Step one is to read the poem aloud." So he had us read a number of poems out loud in class: Shakespeare sonnets, Emily Dickinson poems, and one by Langston Hughes.

He began the next class by stating: "Our second step is to unpack what the poem is about. Often there is the surface meaning and then the various meanings operating under the surface. Pay attention to metaphors, similes, and analogies."

So we each took one of the previous poems we'd read and tried to figure out what was going on. I chose a Shakespeare sonnet, but couldn't get far. It just seemed like he was being overly mushy.

"Step three, pay attention to the rhythm of the poem. It is almost always intentional. Try to figure out why the author is employing the rhythm that he is using." So during the third class he made us read the same poems aloud and discuss how the rhythm was different for each. "Sometimes they are following an accepted formula, other times they are rebelling against established rules."

I was pretty sure I appreciated the ones that rebelled against the rules best.

"Step four," he continued in the next class, "look for enjambment. That is when a sentence or thought does not end with the line of poetry, but continues on to the next line. Typically, enjambed lines of poetry do not have punctuation marks at the end. Consider why this might be. How does it affect how you read it and how you speak it? Listen to what it does to the lines of the poem when spoken aloud."

So we spent a whole class looking for the ways all the poems used enjambment or not. Honestly, I kind of zoned out during that class.

On the fifth class he told us to pay attention to the "literary techniques being deployed." We looked for symbolism, motifs, and repetition. He told us to pay attention to rhymes and something he called "slant rhymes."

After we had those five classes, he said, "Okay, let's pull all five of these steps together to make our toolbox formidable. Let's take a famous poem and employ all five steps." He passed out a poem by bell hooks. When he asked if any of us were familiar with the poem or the poet, Shawn's hand shot up.

"She's actually a relative of mine," he said.

Mr. Snead looked at him suspiciously.

"Seriously?"

"Yes, sir. She's from the Appalachian section of Kentucky. She's my great aunt. I met her at a family wedding a few years ago."

Mr. Snead stared at him for a second, as if wondering whether to believe him. But this was Shawn, so Snead probably knew that he wouldn't be joking about something like this. "Well, if she ever visits you here in Beaver Dam, let me know. It would be great to have her visit the class."

"Yes, sir, I will." Shawn was trying to play it cool, but I could tell he was feeling proud.

After we had spent the class working on the bell hooks poem, Mr. Snead said, "Okay, class, your assignment for this weekend is to analyze a piece of poetry utilizing these tools. You can pick any poem you want—it can even be the lyrics from a famous song, if you wish—and use these five steps. It should be at least two pages in length and is due on Tuesday."

On the bus ride home, I asked Shawn if he was going to write his essay on a bell hooks poem. "And is she really your great aunt?"

Shawn was staring out the window. The mist had finally burned off that afternoon and the sun was shining down for the first time in days. The landscape seemed to sparkle with ice crystals. "I'm not sure if she is a great aunt, a second cousin, or what. We tend to use those terms broadly to cover all relatives. But, yeah, she's family on my momma's side. Her birth name was Gloria Watkins and my momma is a Watkins. But I don't think I'm gonna write on one of her poems. Since he said we could write on song lyrics, I was just thinking about which song I might want to write on."

"Oh yeah! I forgot he said that. I should write my essay on a song."

"Well, people who've had him in the past always suggest writin' on a Bob Dylan song. He seems to have a soft spot for Bob Dylan, but I 'spect half the class is gonna do that. I was thinkin' maybe a Doc Watson song. Maybe even," he gestured out the window to the distant hillside he had pointed out to me weeks before, "'Shady Grove.' It seems highly appropriate."

We rode the rest of the way in silence, both of us thinking about which song we might employ our "formidable toolbox" on.

That night, as I was falling asleep, I had the brilliant idea that I should write about a Lite Brite song. I was so excited, I got out of bed and walked across the cold wooden floor to my desk to write myself a reminder in case I forgot about it in the morning.

I didn't need to worry. I awoke with the perfect song in mind.

"The Unbearable Lightness of Being a Girl" was one of my favorite Lite Brite songs. It was on their first album. Joey had given me a copy of it, knowing I would like it. And that was the song I'd fallen in love with the most. It was a total Grrrl Power song with an insanely catchy chorus:

It's the Unbearable!

Lightness!

The Unbearable Lightness!

Of Being a Girl! Girl! Girl!

I was so excited about the assignment that I spent Saturday afternoon and most of Sunday working on the essay. It ended up being almost four pages long.

I was proud of it. It was so good that even if Mr. Snead hated me, he wouldn't be able to give me a bad grade. I was sure I had a solid A coming my way.

What could possibly go wrong?

5

On Monday morning, when Bethany sauntered in to Mrs. Critcher's class, she looked over at me and smirked. "How's that big ol' head of yours, Vicious Sydney?" I had totally forgotten about the snowball incident from the week before. I shuddered at the memory of the ice running down my back, which caused Bethany's lame friends to break out laughing. So the day was off to a good start.

At lunch, Rita wasn't around when I got to our usual table. Shawn already had a book in front of him and was crunching on a long piece of celery.

"Rita not here?"

"Not yet. How are you doin' with your Snead essay?"

"I'm already finished!" I announced.

Shawn looked up from his book. "Really? Good job."

"No, it's a *great* job! I nailed that bad-boy with my 'formidable toolbox,'" I said, trying my best to imitate Mr. Snead.

Shawn chuckled. "What did you end up writin' on?"

"A Lite Brite song. What about you? Did you end up writing on 'Shady Grove'?"

"Yeah. But I'm still working on it. I discovered two different versions of the song. I couldn't decide which one to use, so I'm writing on both and discussing the differences between them. How slight variations open up different avenues for interpretation."

Man, that kid was a genius.

Just then Rita walked up and joined us. "Hi, guys."

"Hey," I said.

Shawn nodded his greetings and then went back to reading and crunching his celery stalk.

Rita and I engaged in some small talk. I felt like there was some tension there that we were both trying to ignore. That was fine. I didn't want to open any ugly can of worms. I hate worms. Trying not to think about icky, wiggly worms, I managed to finish my sandwich. Then I noticed Ms. Yancey walking by the end of one of the stacks. Oh yeah, my asphalt research! I remembered how she had asked if I would be back today.

I stood up just as Rita looked like she was about to say something to me.

"Excuse me, guys, I gotta go talk to Ms. Yancey about doing a little more research on the computer."

Shawn didn't look up but waved the stub of his celery stalk at me. Rita looked a little hurt but turned back toward her book.

I walked over to where I thought Ms. Yancey would be. Once again, she was re-shelving graphic novels.

"It's no big deal for me to use my own school account," I said as she got up from logging on to the computer. "I don't want to keep bothering you."

"It's no bother. And it's probably best this way." As I sat down, she lingered for a few seconds, as if she was thinking about something. Then she squatted down next to me. "While you are researching asphalt and asphalt plants, you may want to look into the company that is going to build that plant."

"You mean HD Dunkirk Industries?"

She smiled at me, impressed. "Exactly. HD Dunkirk Industries. You may find some interesting things. And you may also want to find out more about who owns that land."

She stood up, patted me awkwardly on the shoulder, and walked back toward the graphic novels.

It didn't take me long to start uncovering information about HD Dunkirk Industries. I started with their website and read the standard promotional information. The company had been formed in the 1920s by Herbert D. Dunkirk, a Texas oil man. Keeping their focus on energy, they expanded into coal mining. The company started to flourish during World War II when it landed a number of contracts supplying the US military with oil and coal. After the war, they also got into road construction by helping build American military bases overseas.

It seemed that they had gotten out of the oil business when they sold off that part of the business to a major oil company in the 1970s. Even though they kept their head-quarters in Houston, today most of their businesses were in the Southeast, where they had a number of coal mines, asphalt plants, and major road construction facilities. They claimed to be the leading paver of roads in at least eight states.

I then turned to doing a media search on HD Dunkirk and I was flooded with newspaper articles and reports by investigative journalists. This was a company with a dirty history. Really dirty. The top articles in my search were all about different lawsuits against the company for pretty horrific environmental disasters they had caused. Coal mines had collapsed, trapping miners underground. There were at least five of those, one in which eight miners had died. In each case, it was claimed that HD Dunkirk had failed to meet basic safety requirements. In each case, they settled the lawsuits out of court and managed to avoid being held responsible by the government. The last mining disaster had been in West Virginia the previous summer and had resulted in several people being injured and one miner paralyzed. I guess the company hadn't learned anything from its past mistakes.

Lawsuits had been filed against it for a wide range of health and safety violations, from the coal miners in West Virginia to a horrible story of one of the bridges they had built collapsing in Tennessee. Plenty of stories reported on the environmental damage caused by their coal mines, by

mountain top removal that poisoned all the nearby waterways, by toxic fumes from their asphalt plants, and on and
on.

The news reports painted a much different picture than
the one on HD Dunkirk's own website, which had pictures
of kids skipping rope on a tree-lined road that I guess the
company had paved. They were presenting themselves as a
family-friendly, environmentally conscious corporation. But
the evidence seemed to suggest the exact opposite.

These guys were really bad.

And they were really powerful. Their website had lots
of photos of the company's CEO shaking hands with past
US presidents (including the current one) and a number of
senators.

There was so much to read about HD Dunkirk, I almost
forgot about Ms. Yancey's suggestion to see who owned the
land that the asphalt plant was going to be built on. It took a
few minutes of searching, but I finally found a small article
about it in the *Franklin Herald,* the regional newspaper.

It said the land was owned by someone named Bradley S.
Winter.

I didn't think I knew who that was. But the name kind of
rang a bell.

As if on cue, the school bell rang.

Rita was waiting for me at our table when I got back from
using the computers. I had Spanish class after lunch on Monday, Wednesday, and Friday. Rita was in the French class that
met right next door, so we walked there together from the
library on those days. I took the fact that she was still waiting
for me as a sign that we were back on good terms.

I grabbed my backpack and quickly shoved the remains
of my lunch in. "Thanks for waiting."

"Sure, but we need to hurry or we're gonna be late." She
started walking out.

"I know, I know. Sorry," I said, grabbing my army jacket off the back of my chair and catching up with her.

"What were you doing, anyway?"

"I've been doing a little research on that asphalt plant they want to build next to the school."

"Huh, sounds thrilling." She chuckled.

"Actually, smarty-*pantalones*, it is!" She laughed, apparently appreciating my lame attempt to impress her with my Spanish. I had taken Latin in Rochester, but they didn't offer that at Beaver Dam. So I had been placed in introductory Spanish. I'd originally been bummed about it, but now I hoped I'd eventually be able to have a conversation in Spanish with Rita. That'd be cool.

"The company behind it is bad news. They've got a horrible record of destroying the environment and putting people at risk, especially their workers." I paused as we got to our classrooms. "Do you know who Bradley S. Winter is?"

As she entered her classroom, Rita looked back at me with an expression that suggested I was the biggest idiot in the school. "Of course. Everybody does."

She left me standing there. Thanks for nothing, I thought.

The late bell rang and I dashed into class.

Bethany and some of her poser posse were in my Spanish class, and as I hurriedly walked to my desk, Bethany called out to the teacher, "Ooooh, Vicious Sydney is *muy tarde!*"

Mrs. Garcia sighed. "That's enough, *Señorita* Winter. Class, take out your quiz book and turn to *la página ochenta tres.*"

And that's when it hit me.

Señorita Winter was Bethany.

Bethany Winter.

Oh, come on.

Shawn filled me in on Bradley Winter on the bus ride home that afternoon. Turns out the Winter family was seriously loaded.

"I don't know their deep history," Shawn said.

"Deep history? What is that supposed to mean?"

"You know, generations back. Where their kin came from or when they got here. But the Winter family has been 'round these parts for a while. There are lots of Winters in and around Beaver Dam. There are two Winters on the county commission. One of them, Stephen Winter, is Bradley Winter's youngest brother. The other, Bobby Winter, is a cousin, I think.

"I think their daddy made most of their money," he continued. "At least, he owned lots of land around Beaver Dam. Bradley Winter is the oldest of the three brothers and he inherited most of it. He probably owns most of the buildings downtown. He's easily the biggest landlord in town. With Stephen Winter probably the second biggest. He's the one who owns the new strip mall with the Harris Teeter."

"That figures," I said, thinking about how much Granny hated that grocery store. I had always thought she was just being cranky, but now I hated it too. "What about Bethany?"

"Bethany is Bradley Winter's only child, so she'll probably inherit his vast fortune. Which'll make her the richest person in Beaver Dam. And don't think she doesn't know it."

"Dang, as if I needed more reasons to hate her," I said, laughing. I looked out the window and thought about what Shawn had said. The Winters sounded crazy rich. Well, at least two of the brothers were. I turned back to Shawn. "You mentioned that there were three brothers, Bradley being the eldest and Stephen the youngest. But what about the middle brother?"

"Ahh, that'd be Walter Winter, but everybody calls him Buster. Like most middle children, he was the rebel. The outcast." He smiled for some reason. "The black sheep of the family."

"I already think he's my favorite of the bunch. What did he do, something scandalous?"

"Very scandalous. He fell in love with someone the family didn't approve of. So they cut him off completely. They took away everything he had: his job, his house, his money. But he didn't care. He married the woman he loved and now they live happily in Atlanta."

"Oh, man, I love this guy."

Shawn turned to me with a huge smile on his face. "Yeah, I love my uncle Buster too."

Oh, snap.

My face was freezing as I trudged up the driveway to Granny and Grandpop's house. As soon as I opened the door, the warm kitchen air made my nose start running and my eyes water. Granny's eyes were watering and her nose was running too, but that was because she was chopping onions. I could see she was making one of her yummy vegetable stews. She wiped her eyes with her apron and told me that Mom was upstairs in bed with a migraine.

"She's been up there all day, poor missy. I think it must be a doozy."

"I'll just stay down here then, if that is okay with you."

"Of course, precious. You're always welcome. Oh, and you got a letter today. Now where did I put it?" It wasn't on the table, so she looked around on the kitchen counters before finding it in her apron pocket.

I hadn't heard from Kris for a while. But it wasn't from her.

It was from Dani.

Hi Sydney!! Thanks so much for your letter. It was great to hear from you. Letter writing is so much fun! I'm so happy you've already found some friends. We'd love to come visit you if we ever get the chance! It sounds beautiful there. We're working on a new album right now! We've recorded most of it. Just still need to do some of the vocals and then mix it. I'll send you a copy of it when it's finished. Joey told me you don't have email or a social media presence (good for you!!!), so I'll mail you a vinyl version. I hope you have access to a turntable! Since you also asked, when I was in school I really liked my English and science classes. I was okay in history. I found it interesting but could never remember the names of kings and presidents, or keep all the important dates in my head! I was way more into reading literature and finding out how stuff worked in biology, chemistry, and physics. In fact, I still use chemistry almost every day. I'm a baker at a vegan restaurant here in Chicago. I do all the breads and desserts. The worst part of the job is that I have to go in around six a.m. to start baking. But otherwise it is a great job. I get to experiment and come up with new types of vegan desserts. That's where my chemistry background comes in handy! Plus, they are cool with me taking huge chunks of time off when I go on tour. And when I go in early in the morning, I'm usually the only one there, so I get to blast my own music in the kitchen. Which are your favorite classes? Are there any good books you are reading? I'm always on the lookout for new books, so send me your recommendations. Talk to you soon!

xoxo DANI

Again, she signed it with a little heart over the *I* in her name. I guess that was her thing.

And at the bottom of the page she drew another picture. This one was a self-portrait of her as a baker, with an apron, a big chef's hat (with an arrow pointing to the hat saying "I don't really wear one of these!") and a huge spoon in her hand.

After reading it a few times, I dug some paper out of my backpack and wrote her a long letter back. I told her about Mr. Snead's class, his poetry appreciation assignment, and how I had written my essay on Lite Brite's "The Unbearable Lightness of Being a Girl." I probably bored her with the summary of my paper, but I was so excited to share this news with her.

I told her about how I was getting used to life at Beaver Dam, but that I still missed everything back in Rochester. Especially Kris and Joey.

I don't know why, but I also told her about the proposed asphalt plant near the school and some of the things I had learned about asphalt and HD Dunkirk Industries. I guess I was getting a little obsessed with it, because I spent one whole side of a page talking about asphalt! When I finished, I had filled up both sides of four pages. I can't remember ever writing Kris that long of a letter.

Granny had left while I was writing, but the smell of her slow-cooking stew filled the kitchen. I was just putting my letter in an envelope when Mom shuffled into the kitchen. She was in her robe and had dark circles under her eyes.

"Oh, hey, sweetheart," she said. "I didn't hear you come in. Did you just get home?"

"No, I've been here for almost an hour. I didn't want to bother you. Sorry your head hurts."

Mom groaned and then said, "Do you usually get home at that time? I guess I'm never around in the afternoon." She was rooting around in the fridge, looking for something.

"Yeah, the bus drops me off right out front. Did you have classes today?"

"I skipped them. I was up late last night working on an assignment, but when I got up this morning I had this horrible migraine. Sydney, do we have any soda? I need more caffeine for my head, but the coffee I've been drinking is killing my stomach."

"There are a couple of cans of RC Cola on the door." We always had RC in the fridge because Granny and Grandpop split a can with their lunch every day.

Mom looked over and picked one out of the fridge door.

"Thank god. Caffeine is the only thing that seems to help." She opened the can and took a long sip.

I thought for a second. Mom had grown up here in Beaver Dam. Bethany and I were the same age. So that probably meant that Mom was around the same age as Bradley Winter, or one of his brothers. "Mom, did you go to school with Bradley Winter?" I asked.

She was still drinking from the can, but almost sprayed RC across the kitchen. She ran to the sink and managed to swallow what was in her mouth, while keeping from coughing. "Oh my god," she exclaimed once she got herself under control. "Why in the world would you ask me that?"

"Well, his daughter Bethany is in my class. I just thought you might have known him growing up."

"Geez, I haven't thought of the Winter boys in ages." She

stared out the window above the sink for a few moments. "What's she like, his daughter?"

"Bethany? Pretty horrible, actually. She seems like a spoiled rich brat. Really conceited and full of herself. And she's got this pack of carbon-copied zombie friends that follow her everywhere."

"Figures," Mom mumbled to herself, still staring out the window.

I watched her for at least a minute and she didn't move. Finally I cleared my throat. "So, I guess that means you knew the Winter brothers?"

The sound of my voice seemed to break her out of her trance. She looked down at the RC can in her hand, as if wondering how it got there. "Knew them? Yeah, I knew them." She paused and then added, "Bradley and I dated all through high school. We were engaged to be married when I met your father."

Holy crudola.

6

I turned in my poetry appreciation essay the next day, but I spent most of the morning lost in a fog.

Mom had dated Bradley Winter. They had been engaged to be married. They must have been in love at one point. It was weird thinking about Mom being in love with someone besides Dad. But it was even weirder realizing that if they had gotten married, then I might have been Bethany Winter's sister. Or maybe I would have been Bethany. It was mind boggling.

But it also helped me understand a few things better. I had discovered a missing piece to the jigsaw puzzle that was my mom. Joey and I could never understand why she had been so tough on Dad before he was killed. I mean, most of her complaints were spot on. He was an idealistic musician who lived with his head in the clouds, thinking about music and songs. But that was just who he was, you know. It wasn't like he could change how he was built. We always thought it was unfair of Mom to expect him to be something he wasn't. Surely she knew what she was getting when they got married.

Now I realized that it was less about who Dad was than who he wasn't. She had been engaged to the wealthiest guy in her hometown, from a family who was absolutely loaded. Like Buster, she had walked away from the Winters' fortune for love. But unlike Buster, it wasn't happily ever after. I wonder if Mom had regretted marrying Dad. She had given up the promise of wealth and influence for the idealistic dreaming of an aspiring musician. Not only had Dad not been much of a success as a musician or as a breadwinner, but he had gone and gotten himself killed.

That had to have been tougher on Mom than I had imagined.

When I got to the library for lunch, I told Shawn and Rita what I had learned about my mom and her past life with Bradley Winter. They listened intently, Shawn not even picking up a book. "Wow," he said. "So if your mom had married Bradley Winter, then that woulda made you…"

"I know, I know," I interrupted. "I would be Bethany. Or she would be me. I've already thought about that. It's enough to make me puke."

"Actually, I was gonna say that it woulda made us cousins."

"Hey, yeah," I said. "I hadn't thought about that. That's pretty cool." We grinned at each other.

"That's crazy," Rita said. "But how did you find out about this? Did your mom just tell you out of the blue?"

"No, I was asking her about Bradley Winter. I found out about him because he owns the land that they want to build the asphalt plant on."

"He owns half this town," Shawn said.

"I know. He's my landlord," Rita replied.

"What?" I exclaimed.

"Yeah, he owns the apartment building my family lives in. We have one of the first-floor units downtown on Vine Street. It's a pretty crappy apartment. The ceiling leaks from the shower upstairs. The heat never works properly. It's pretty cold and drafty. But it's like that in all the apartments."

"You should complain," I said.

"We have, but nothing gets done."

"Then report him to the police."

Shawn scoffed from behind his book. "This is Bradley Winter you're talking 'bout. The most powerful man in Beaver Dam."

"Plus," Rita said after a moment, "we're all migrant families in the building. My family is legal, but I'm not sure if everyone else is. It's always best not to get the police involved if you are Hispanic. That draws attention and they might start deporting people."

"What? That's crazy!"

"That's America," Shawn said. "Especially if your skin has some pigmentation in it."

I didn't know what to say. Sure, I knew about racism in America. I'd encountered plenty of it in Rochester, such as seeing graffiti with racial slurs or from school kids being cruel to each other. But I'd never known anybody who was afraid to go to the police. At least, I didn't think I did.

I thought about my old friends back home and wondered if some of them lived with the fear of deportation. Or if they lived in crappy apartments because of where their families came from. I had never thought about it before.

I felt a wave of powerlessness wash over me. Here I was with a friend who lived in what sounded like a horrible apartment building. Her landlord was the most powerful person in the area, with two relatives on the city commission, and therefore untouchable. And he was working with what seemed like an evil corporation to put a dangerous asphalt plant right near my school.

And it didn't seem like there was anything I could do about any of it.

That afternoon I finally got a letter from Kris. She seemed genuinely excited that I had gotten a letter from Dani of Lite Brite. But she spent most of her letter telling me about all of the cool shows that I was missing. Plus, a new family had moved into the neighborhood with two kids a grade above us. They were twins, a girl named Stefanie and a guy named Stuart. Kris talked about how cool they were. It seemed they were hanging out a lot with my old group of friends. I felt a pang of jealousy, but I tried to be excited when I wrote her back. I told Kris about my second letter from Dani, the essay

I had written about the Lite Brite song for Mr. Snead, Bethany's bullying, and a bit about the proposed asphalt plant.

I was clearly getting obsessed with asphalt.

When Grandpop asked if I wanted to join him on a trip into town before dinner, I agreed. He was going to the hardware store and Harris Teeter. I asked him if we could drive by the school on the way in.

"Sure, it's a little out of the way, but it's a nice enough afternoon for a drive."

It was a beautiful afternoon, especially for late February. There wasn't a cloud in the sky and the sun was warmer than usual. The road was covered with little streams of water from the melting snowbanks on the sides of the road. The dripping ice on the trees sparkled in the sunlight. Back in Rochester, the snow would have been dirty and almost black from the pollution, but here it was, well, snow white.

Man, I had never realized that Rochester was so dirty.

As we neared the school and the site of the proposed asphalt plant, I asked Grandpop to slow down. "I just want to read this sign more clearly," I told him.

Grandpop pulled the truck over at the gate's entrance so we could read the sign. The smaller writing underneath listed a bunch of proposed ordinance numbers and stated that there would be a public hearing in early March. "What does it mean, a public hearing?" I asked him.

"It means the zoning committee for the county will hold a meeting open to the public to consider whether they should allow this asphalt plant to be built."

"So, anyone can get up to speak?"

"Yeah, s'pose so," he said, putting the truck back in gear and gently pulling back onto the road. "But it won't make a lick of difference."

"Why not?"

"Because all this land belongs to the Winter family," he said, gesturing out the window. "And the head of the zoning committee is little Stephen Winter. So that proposal is gonna get approved no matter what."

I looked out the window as we were passing the school. The parking lot was empty except for a few cars that I guess belonged to teachers staying late. "Do the Winters own the school, too?"

"Oh no," Grandpop said, laughing. "But they pulled some strings to get the school built out here. Old Man Winter bought this stretch of land years ago. Got it real cheap 'cause it seemed worthless and inaccessible. Too rocky to farm on, too remote to develop."

"But there is a road right here," I pointed out, as if he hadn't noticed the wide smooth thing that we were driving upon called Laurel Ridge Road.

"Well, there is now. Old Man Winter spent years lobbyin' the folks down in Raleigh to build this so-called bypass into Beaver Dam. It just loops off the main road and rejoins it before you enter town, right where the new Harris Teeter is. Laurel Ridge is a useless road that nobody needed and it cost a fortune. Nobody wanted it, but Old Man Winter used his political connections to get it built. Rumor has it he made some big political donations. Even promised to get the road built cheaply, which turned out to be a lie."

"By who?" I asked, thinking that it had to have been HD Dunkirk Industries. I started to suspect that the Winters and Dunkirk Industries were pretty darn cozy.

"Beats me. But buildin' this road suddenly made all of the land the Winters owned out here very valuable. The school was one of the first things they built. And since they built this new Harris Teeter here," he said as he pulled into the parking lot, "I suspect there is gonna be a lot more development on Laurel Ridge in the comin' years. That's one thing I'll say for them Winters, they know how to make their money make money."

After we got all the groceries on the list, we drove further into town where the old hardware store was. First we pulled into an old convenience store and Grandpop bought us each an RC Cola and fried fruit pies. "Your granny don't need to know about these," he said as he climbed back into the truck, passing me a bottle and a pie. "Lottie would give us an endless mountain of grief if she knew we were eatin' fried pies before dinner. So let's just eat 'em here and destroy the evidence."

"That works for me."

The pie was delicious. It was a fried peach pie. I knew from past trips in the summertime how delicious they were. Eating this one made me forget how much I missed the vegan doughnuts Kris and I would occasionally get on our walk home from school.

I don't care what you say. A fried peach pie beats a doughnut hands down any day.

It turned out the hardware store didn't have what Grandpop needed—some type of tubing he wanted for an irrigation system he was trying to rig up in the greenhouse. Gardening was Grandpop's primary activity. Mom told me that when he was a young man, he had worked construction until a huge rafter landed on his left leg, which is why he walked with a slight limp. That ended his building career, but he'd been lucky enough to score a job as an inspector for the town of Beaver Dam once he recovered. But now that he was retired, he spent most of his time in the greenhouse or the gardens.

"No big deal," he said as we climbed back into the truck. "I can get the tubing from the garden-supply company over in Franklin. I'm sure they'll have what I need. I'll give your momma a ride to the university and get it then."

An idea came to me. "Can it wait a few days?"

"Sure. Ain't like I need the part any time soon. Why?"

"Well, if you can wait until Saturday, I could go with you.

You could drop me off downtown. I hear there is a record store that is supposed to be good."

"The one next to the bookstore on King Street?"

"I guess so. Is there more than one record store in Franklin?" I asked, getting excited at the possibility. I hadn't walked through a record or bookstore since leaving Rochester. It had been Kris and my favorite activity.

Grandpop laughed. "No, I guess there isn't. Sure, if it's all right with your momma, we can go in on Saturday. We can grab us some lunch and make a day of it."

I hadn't been out of Beaver Dam in almost two months. Franklin was a little less than an hour away, and even though Mom drove there to take classes, I hadn't been yet. Mom said it was minuscule compared to Rochester, but I knew it had to be bigger than Beaver Dam. Pretty much any place would be.

When I mentioned to Rita and Shawn that I was going on Saturday, they acted like I was going to New York City.

"If you go out to lunch, there are some great Mexican restaurants there," Rita said. "Well, no, they're not that great. Actually, they're not very good at all. A few are passable, I guess. But since there are no Mexican restaurants in Beaver Dam, they are better than nothing."

"They have a delicious Indian restaurant that does a nice lunch buffet," Shawn said. "The bhindi masala is quite good."

Rita and I both looked at him.

"What? The Black kid can't appreciate Indian food?"

I laughed. "No, it's just that you eat nothing but peanut butter and jelly sandwiches, celery, and carrots for lunch, every single day."

Shawn took a bite of his celery stick, making sure to crunch it as loud as possible. "Celery is cool. And I like what I like. I especially like okra, which is the main ingredient of bhindi masala, which you probably didn't know."

"Yes, I did!" I replied in a pretend huff.

I hadn't.

"But more important, can you try to find a few books for me?" continued Shawn. "Here, I'll give you a list." He ripped out a page from his notebook and started writing.

"Uh, sure, I guess," I said, looking at his growing list with concern.

"Oh, me too!" said Rita, as she took out her own piece of paper.

"Whoa, how much is this gonna cost me?" I laughed.

"I'll give you some money. I'll rank the books and just buy the ones that you can find until the money runs out," Shawn said as he started a second column.

"Can you just get one or two from this list and I'll pay you back?" Rita said a little sheepishly as she handed me a list with five titles on it.

"Sure, no problem." I folded up the list and slipped it into my backpack.

It was snowing slightly when Grandpop and I drove into Franklin on Saturday morning. Mom was with us, because she wanted to spend the day in the university library. Granny didn't want to go, so the three of us squeezed into Grandpop's truck. I rode in the middle where Grandpop would occasionally whack me in the knee when he shifted gears.

We dropped Mom off at the university library and then drove to lunch. We decided to try out a Mexican restaurant that Mom had said was pretty good. It wasn't. I used to eat burritos all the time in Rochester and these couldn't hold a tamale to them.

Then Grandpop dropped me off at Cherryhill Books and Records. It was in an old building on the edge of downtown. It turned out to be one business made up of two separate rooms with a big opening between them. The books were in one room and the records in the other. I guess at one time it had been two separate stores, but then they took out part of the dividing wall between them.

I decided to get the books first, knowing that I might lose myself in the records if I started there.

Shawn had given me twenty dollars but it took me a while to work down his list. I was on the second column before I found three books that together cost a little over twenty dollars. I then turned to Rita's list. I found three of the five books she listed and decided to buy them all. I knew she could reimburse me for only two of them. I'd give the other one to her as a gift. As I was hunting down their books, I also found the newest book in the *Cricklewood* series. I was a big fan and I didn't even know a new book had come out, so I just had to buy it.

I spent so much time looking for books, I worried I'd be rushed when I got to the record side of the building. There were only vinyl records there, which was perfect for me. I preferred to collect vinyl even though I didn't have my own record player anymore. Back home, Dad had had a turntable hooked up to his stereo system that he let me use. He'd even shown me how to make digital versions of whatever record I wanted. Mom had sold the stereo, along with all our furniture, when she sold the house. I knew Granny and Grandpop had an old record player at their house, but I hadn't seen anyone use it.

The record store had vinyl bins along all the walls, and then one long double-sided bin running in the middle of the room. It was about half the size of the bookstore side, but it still looked pretty impressive. Two other customers were flipping through the records. They both looked like college students. Every few minutes they would call to each other and hold up a record cover to show the other. After about five minutes they walked out without buying anything.

There was an older guy behind the counter. He had a big beard and a shaved head, and he was wearing an old Hüsker Dü shirt. He had given me a nod when I walked in. I was getting a fellow Ravenclaw vibe. I worked my way through the bins on one wall. It was mostly funk, reggae, and R&B. After a few minutes I started working on the records on the middle aisle.

"That's a cool shirt," the guy behind the counter said.

I looked down to see what shirt I was wearing. "Thanks. It's by a band called Lite Brite."

"Yeah, I figured. That's the logo they used on their first album."

I was stunned. Here was someone who not only knew who Lite Brite was, but could recognize their logo. "Uh, you know about them?"

"Yeah," he said, walking out from behind the counter. "I think we have both the debut album and their follow-up EP over here. By the way, you are in the Classic Rock section. That's where most of the college kids go, tryin' to find copies of Pink Floyd albums. But the alternative, indie and punk stuff is against this wall." He looked over at me and gave a knowing smile. "It's where we keep the good stuff."

I walked over to where he was standing, as he pulled out the Lite Brite debut and EP. "Yep, one copy of each. But I'm guessin' you probably have both already, am I right?"

"Oh yeah. They're my favorite band."

"Right on. You obviously have excellent taste."

"I can't wait for their next album."

"I don't know if there is going to be one anytime soon. I haven't heard anything about it."

"They are finishing recording it right now. It's supposed to be done by early summer," I said, adding in what I hoped was a nonchalant way, "Dani DeLite told me."

He gave me a surprised look and then laughed. "Get out of town! Are you for real? You know Dani DeLite?"

"Well, kind of. We're like pen pals or something. She knows my brother Joey and she started writing to me when I moved to Beaver Dam."

"You live in Beaver Dam?"

"I do now. I'm originally from Rochester, New York, but my mom dragged me down here when she moved back home to Beaver Dam. We live with my grandparents now."

"Well, welcome to the neighborhood. And thanks for makin' the drive over from Beaver Dam."

"My grandpop drove me. I'm too young to drive."

The guy laughed. "Yeah, I figured." He held out his hand. "I'm Ben. This is my store. Nice to meet you."

"Sydney. Sydney Talcott," I replied, shaking his hand and looking around. "You own this whole store? I'd love to own this many records."

"I co-own this half of the store with a buddy of mine. And two other friends own the bookstore side. And to be honest with you, most of the records in here are pretty crappy." He laughed. "But we know our clientele and we try to cater to 'em. The college kids love the classic rock and the reggae. We've got a nice section of bluegrass and old-time music in the back for the local crowd. And a smattering of stuff for the curious tourist who comes in."

"Tourists come in here to buy records?"

"Well, we get a lot of tourists in Franklin during the summer. But when it's foggy and rainy, they can't enjoy their outdoor mountain activities. They walk around King Street and are always amazed to see a real live record store still in existence. Actually, the tourists are pretty good customers 'cause most tend to buy at least one album, mostly for the novelty of buyin' a record while on vacation."

I started flipping through the records in the bins next to the Lite Brite records. "Whoa, you've got a pretty good selection here. Latterman! Le Tigre! Lemuria!"

"Dang, you do have good taste," said Ben, acting impressed.

I responded in my best Elvis voice, "Thank you. Thank you very much."

We chatted for the next fifteen minutes as I flipped

through the records. There were several I knew about but had never seen physical copies of before. But many were new to me. When I found an album or band I loved, I would tell Ben. Sometimes he'd make suggestions of other bands that were similar.

As I got to the end of the alternative/indie/punk section, the heavy metal section started. "Ugh. I'm not really into metal," I said.

"Can't say I blame you. Too much devil worshipping?" he said, laughing.

"Less that it's such a dude show."

He laughed again. "I know exactly what you mean. A lot of it is toxic masculinity set to music."

"I know, right?"

"Well, this last crate is for local bands and musicians," said Ben, pointing to the section next to the check-out counter. "It's definitely worth checking out. But just a warning: we treat all local acts equally and list everything alphabetically, rather than by genre. So you'll find local bluegrass acts alongside some of the college rock bands in there."

I started flipping through the records.

The front door chimed as Grandpop walked in. "Hey, sweetpea, you 'bout ready to head back?"

"Sure, Grandpop. Just one second, let me finish this last crate. Grandpop, this is Ben. Ben, this is my grandpop."

"How ya doin'?" said Ben as he shook Grandpop's hand.

"Good, good. I haven't been in this place since it was, what, a pharmacy?"

"Actually, this side was a florist and the bookstore side was the pharmacy…" Grandpop and Ben chatted away about the various businesses that had occupied the storefronts on this block. After looking at the last record, I turned to leave.

"Hold up, Sydney. Here is something for you." Ben reached back into the crate of local releases and pulled out an album. I had noticed that there were three copies of that album. On the cover was an intricate black and white drawing of a skull with a huge beard and little designs tucked into the beard. At the top were the words *The Ward Cleavers*.

"This is my band. I know the cover looks like we're a metal band, but we're not. Just old-school punk spiced with some local flavoring. Think The Ramones mixed with Earl Scruggs."

"Who's Earl Scruggs?" I said.

Ben shot Grandpop a glance and they both started laughing. Grandpop said, "Clearly I am not doing a good job on her musical education."

I looked at each of them confused. Ben added, "He's probably the greatest banjo player who ever lived. Don't worry, he's pretty punk rock."

I tried to pay him for the record, but he waved me off. "No, no. That's a gift. Just come back and let me know what you thought of it. But you need to pay for those books on the other side. We keep our registers separate."

I thanked him and headed over to the other side. He waved out the window as we drove away.

So lunch had sucked but the record and bookstore were great. I'll take that over a decent burrito any day.

7

When we got home, Grandpop cleaned off his record player so that I could listen to my new Ward Cleavers record. The turntable was an ancient thing that even had a 78 rpm setting, in addition to the standard 33 1/3 and 45 speeds. It was in the front room of the house, on a shelf surrounded by dusty old books. I didn't even know there were speakers in that room until I heard music coming out of them. I had mistaken them for big ugly boxes on the top shelf, but they sounded a lot fuller and louder than the little wireless speaker I used with my MP3 player.

Turns out there were dozens and dozens of old records in a cabinet under the turntable. Grandpop pulled out some Earl Scruggs, along with a few others he thought I should listen to, including a couple of Doc Watson records. He told me I could listen to anything else I wanted to. But mostly I listened to the Ward Cleavers, keeping the volume down low enough that it wouldn't bother Granny.

They were awesome!

Ben, listed as Ben Cleaver, played guitar and sang. Dexter Cleaver played bass and Sarah Cleaver was their drummer. But Ben shared vocal duties on most songs with Betty Cleaver, who also played fiddle, banjo, and mandolin. Honestly, I thought the songs she sang lead on were way better than his. Sorry, Ben.

At first it was weird hearing punk songs with banjos and fiddles. But by the end of the first side, I was totally into it. It made the music sound unique.

On the second side, there was an amazing song called "Mountain Laurel." With a voice that was surprisingly sweet, compared to the more aggressive singing on other songs, Betty sang the chorus:

We gotta protect what nature gave us

'Cause there ain't nobody gonna save us.

I fear for the days that are comin'

When there won't be no mountain laurels bloomin'.

After several listens, "Mountain Laurel" was definitely my favorite song on the album. It got under my skin and I was humming the tune throughout dinner. So that evening, after I helped Grandpop clean up the dinner dishes, I put the album on one more time and took out a piece of paper.

I decided to write to the mayor of Beaver Dam, urging him not to allow the building of the asphalt plant. I started the letter explaining that I was a student at the middle school and the plant would have a direct impact on the students. I also talked about the need for us to preserve the region's natural resources, pointing out how beautiful it was in Beaver Dam and how we needed to protect the environment not just for the tourists who came to see the mountains but for our children and grandchildren. Finally, I mentioned a few things I had learned about HD Dunkirk Industries, suggesting that they didn't have the best track record when it came to taking care of people or the environment.

The next day was Sunday, which usually meant Joey called in the late afternoon. Letters from Kris were pretty rare now. I told myself that she was probably just getting busy at school, but my feelings were still hurt. In my darker moments, I imagined her hanging out with our old friends and forgetting all about me.

But Joey's calls were like clockwork.

Sure enough, right before dinner, the phone rang. Mom talked with him for a few minutes and then she handed me the phone.

"Hey, kiddo, what's going on?" he asked.

"Oh, you know. Living the dream."

He laughed. "That bad, huh?"

"Actually, things are pretty cool." I told him about my trip into Franklin and meeting Ben. He had never heard of the Ward Cleavers but was interested to hear some "authentic mountain punk," as he called it. I promised to send him a copy, if I could figure out how to record it using Grandpop's ancient turntable.

"No worries. As we were talking, I looked them up on the internet and I'm downloading their album now. It looks interesting." I was always stoked to turn Joey on to some band that he hadn't heard before.

"Check out the song 'Mountain Laurel.' It's my favorite on the album," I added. "Oh, and I got another letter from Dani DeLite! She is so awesome!"

"She really is," agreed Joey. "I knew you'd hit it off with Dani. She seemed like a thirteen-year-old at heart. When they were here, all she wanted to do was find out where the best ice cream and pinball machines were! That whole band are super cool. Before the show they took me to a trampoline park. It was so much fun."

We talked a bit about other bands he had seen in Buffalo and the classes he was taking. I told him about my Lite Brite essay for Mr. Snead, as well as the letter I had written to the mayor about the asphalt plant.

"Good luck fighting The Man!" he joked. "No, seriously. That's great that you're getting involved. We need more people like you in this world."

It was so good talking with Joey. I hung up with a familiar feeling of happiness and sadness mixed together. I was learning that that is what homesickness felt like.

On Monday morning, I earned my second trip to the principal's office. Again, it wasn't my fault. I was sitting at my desk, waiting for social studies to start and minding my own business, reading an old *Lumberjanes*. Suddenly the comic was snatched out of my hands. I turned around to see Bethany waving it in the air.

"Oooh, look everybody. Vicious Sydney is readin' a comic book. Aren't they a bit old for you? Shouldn't you stick with Dr. Seuss?"

I jumped up from my desk and pushed past her laughing lame-oid friends.

It was one of the early issues of *Lumberjanes*, so it was pretty valuable to me.

"Give it back, Bethany. Now!"

"What are you gonna do, get vicious on me?"

"You need to work on your routine, Bethany. That shtick is getting tired." I reached out for my comic book. "You're being a jerk. Give it back. Now."

She held the comic above her head, taunting me. She stood a couple of inches taller than me, so the *Lumberjanes* was just out of my reach. I grabbed her arm with all my strength and pulled it down.

"Ouch!" Bethany cried out. But I didn't care. I wrenched the comic out of her hand. And I may or may not have used a swear word comparing Bethany to a female dog. It's kind of a blur. But as luck would have it, Mrs. Critcher chose just that moment to walk into the classroom. She was pretty sure I had used such a word. Luckily she hadn't seen me yank on Bethany's arm or I might have gotten in real trouble. But while she ignored Bethany's pathetic request to go to the ER or at least see the nurse, she sent me to the principal's office for swearing.

It was so unfair.

I waited outside Mrs. Fletcher's office for ten minutes, memorizing all the motivational posters she had on her wall. They were mostly about cats hanging in there. Eventually I was summoned into her office.

Mrs. Fletcher sat behind a huge desk covered with papers

and binders. Her gray hair was cut fairly short, and reading glasses hung around her neck by a beaded chain. Her business suit was probably fashionable a decade before. I'm being generous. Maybe two decades.

When I met her on my first day at Beaver Dam Middle, Mrs. Fletcher had been like a warm, welcoming grandmother. When Mr. Snead had sent me down a few weeks ago, she had given me a warning like a concerned grandmother. Now she was in angry, mean grandmother mode. "Let me be clear from the beginning, Miss Talcott. This behavior is simply not acceptable in my school."

"But, ma'am, don't you want to know what happened?"

"No," she snapped. "Frankly, I don't."

"But Bethany was bullying me. She—"

"Please," Mrs. Fletcher interrupted. "Bethany Winter is a sweet, respectable young lady who would never hurt a fly."

I opened and then closed my mouth, as my brain tried to compute whether or not we were talking about the same Bethany Winter. It probably looked like I was doing an impression of a fish.

"Now, I don't know how they did things back in New York." The way she pronounced "New York" made it clear that she did not hold the state in high regard. "But swearing and abusive behavior toward fellow students is simply not allowed here in Beaver Dam."

More fish imitations from me.

"This is your second violation. While I would normally allow students three strikes, it seems to me that such latitude would be lost on you. You need to understand that such behavior is simply unacceptable in my school. I will be contacting your parents about this matter." She was glowering, focusing all of her grandmother anger at me. "And if I hear of another incident of you misbehaving, swearing, or bullying Bethany or any other child here at Beaver Dam, so help me, Miss Talcott..." She trailed off, letting me know that it was probably best she didn't complete that sentence.

I mumbled underneath my breath, "This is bogus."

"What was that?" she snapped.

"Nothing."

"I would hope so. Do we have an understanding, Miss Talcott?"

"Yes, ma'am."

Me, bullying Bethany? Was it Ultimate Bizarro Day and nobody told me?

For the rest of the morning, I fumed about the injustice of getting in trouble for being bullied by Bethany. People were whispering and snickering about me in the hallways. When I got to the library for lunch, both Rita and Shawn's backpacks sat at our table, but they were nowhere to be seen. After a few moments, they walked up with several books in their arms, laughing. They stopped when they saw me.

"Hey, Sydney," said Shawn. "We heard about what happened to you this morning. Everyone's talking about it."

I felt my cheeks turn hot from embarrassment. It was bad enough that everybody was talking about me, but to have my so-called friends laughing at my expense was too much. "Oh, so you think my suffering is funny?" I snapped, shooting them an angry look. Rita recoiled a bit, as if she had just seen a rattlesnake.

"No, not at all. We weren't laughing at you," she replied, stunned.

"Then what was so funny?"

"Actually, we were joking about some of the things we could do to Bethany," she replied.

Adjusting his glasses, Shawn added, "I was sayin' we could replace her shampoo with hair remover. How funny would it be if she woke up bald?"

Rita giggled a little and then stopped. "I know I shouldn't wish bad things on people, but she is just so horrible."

I felt my anger fading away. At least they realized what an awful person Bethany was. I told them what Mrs. Fletcher said, about how Bethany was a sweet and respectable girl who wouldn't hurt a fly. They cracked up and Shawn almost choked on his sandwich from laughing so hard.

"You know," I said thoughtfully. "Bethany would be way more interesting with a bald head."

"You would think that," Rita said.

"Even better, we could dye each of her minions' hair a different color; that way we could tell them apart."

We all laughed until Ms. Yancey stuck her head around a corner and shushed us.

We apologized and started reading our books. But then a thought occurred to me. I don't think anyone had ever told me the names of Bethany's friends.

"What are their names, anyway?" I asked.

"Whose?" said Rita.

"Those clones that hang around Bethany all the time. Especially those two girls. They're like carbon copies. How does anyone tell them apart?"

Rita suppressed a giggle and Shawn pushed his glasses up his nose as if to get a better look at me.

"What?" I asked.

"Um, Sydney. You do realize that they are twins, don't you?"

Oh, crud. I hadn't. I don't know why I had never noticed that before. I just assumed they were all just carbon copies within a cliquey club. I don't know how I hadn't realized they actually really looked alike. Now that I thought about it, I realized that the two girls were identical twins.

I'm sure my eyes must have gone really wide as the realization dawned on me. There was a long silence and then we all fell out laughing again.

Ms. Yancey stuck her head around another corner and shushed us even louder.

We apologized again and went back to reading and eating our lunches. After a few minutes, I remembered about the books I had gotten for them in Franklin.

"I had a hard time finding most of the ones on your list," I said to Shawn as I passed his books to him, "but I did find these three." He actually squealed with glee.

"And, Rita, I was able to get these three for you as well." Her face had been excited, but now I noticed a dark cloud pass across it.

"Um, I only have money for two. I'll have to get you the rest of the money later this week. Maybe next week."

"Don't worry about it. The third book is on me. I got Shawn three books and didn't want you to feel left out."

"Thanks, but I'll pay you back for all of these," she said with determination.

"Don't worry about it, it's my treat."

"No," Rita snapped, getting angry. "I can pay for them. I'll give you the money in a few days."

I started to argue with her but caught Shawn's eye. He had been peering at me over his book, and the look he gave me let me know that I should drop it. I guess I had annoyed Rita by buying her more books than she had asked for. I didn't think it was a big deal. In fact, I thought I was being generous, but it seemed like I had upset her.

I changed the subject by mentioning the letter I wrote to the mayor.

They both stopped reading. Shawn looked thoughtful for a second. If anything, Rita looked even more annoyed than she had before. "Why would you do that?"

"Duh! Because the asphalt plant is a crappy idea. It's going to mess up the environment around here."

"Are you sure writing to the mayor is a good idea? Why would you want to get involved like that?"

I looked at her in disbelief. "Because they are going to build it near our school. It is going to affect all of us. Me, you, Shawn. All of us!"

Shawn interjected, speaking softly. "I'm not sayin' you're wrong about the asphalt plant, Sydney. But I'm not sure a letter to the mayor is gonna have much of an impact."

"Why not?" I asked indignantly.

"Well, in Beaver Dam, the mayor doesn't do anything. Our current mayor has been in office for most of my life. All he does is dress up like Santa for the Christmas parade and cut ribbons whenever a new business opens. The county commission has all the real power."

"Oh."

I didn't know that.

I stewed in my grumpy mood on the way home that afternoon. Shawn sat quietly next to me for most of the ride. I could tell he was being careful. After almost fifteen minutes of silence, he said, "Are you still angry 'bout the incident with Bethany this morning?"

I had been replaying the events in my mind, thinking about how I could have reacted differently. But I decided to deflect Shawn's question. "No, not really," I lied. "That fart-knocker isn't worth the time or the energy."

"That's definitely true."

"I was just wondering why Rita was so annoyed at lunch," I said.

"About the books? Well, she's pretty sensitive about her family. It's not that they're poor. It's just that they're not *not* poor, if you know what I mean."

"Well, then what's the big deal? I bought her a book as a gift. It's like an early birthday present."

"Sure, but it's not her birthday, is it?"

"So?"

"Well, to give a birthday gift is understandable. But to give her free books like this just draws her attention to the fact that she doesn't have as much money as you or I do."

"I don't get it. Someone gave me a free record this week-end, and I didn't get all bent out of shape."

"That's 'cause you could have paid for it if you wanted, right?" he said, looking at me as he pushed his glasses back up his nose. "Listen, I get where you're coming from, Syd-ney. You got each of us three books, and since she couldn't pay for all of hers, you gave one of 'em to her as a present. That was a nice thing you did. It really was. But for her, it just reminded her that she doesn't have as much money as we do. You don't have to agree with her, but my advice is to just accept it. I've learned to be extra sensitive about financial matters around Rita. It's just part of being her friend."

I still didn't understand what the big deal was, but I was starting to get it. I thought about making fun of Shawn for using a term like *financial matters* but changed my mind. I didn't need to spend my time bickering with the few friends that I did have. Instead, I asked why Rita reacted the way she did when I mentioned my letter to the mayor.

Shawn sighed. "That's another thing about Rita. Part of her survival strategy is to avoid attention."

"But this asphalt plant is dangerous. Doesn't she get that?"

"I'm sure she does. But the stakes are always going to be different for her. She's an immigrant, we're not."

I went quiet again, looking out the window at the moun-tain laurels on the hillside and thinking.

There was a letter waiting for me when I got home. It was from Kris. Finally. If I was in a bad mood before reading it, I was in a worse one afterwards. It was a page long and all she talked about was the fun she was having with her new twin friends, Stefanie and Stuart. And she spent a good bit of the time telling me how cute Stuart was.

Barf.

I mean, I tried to be understanding. I had new friends too. But they hadn't replaced Kris. She was still my best friend.

But it seemed like she was forgetting about me. And Kris had never shown any interest in boys before. Neither of us did. That gushy, goopy crud was gross and stupid. What the heck was going on? I read the letter again. It didn't even sound like Kris.

In the past, as soon as I got one of her letters I'd always written Kris back immediately. But this time, I put the letter on my desk and went back downstairs to listen to some records on Grandpop's turntable.

The Ward Cleavers seemed too upbeat for my mood. I flipped through some of Grandpop's records that he had pulled out for me. I put on a Doc Watson album. About halfway through, I recognized one of the songs. It was "Shady Grove," the song that Shawn had sung and written his essay about it. It was good. Really good. It gave me goosebumps. I restarted the whole record, paying more attention to it this time.

Reading the liner notes confirmed what I had guessed from the photo on the front. Doc Watson was blind. But man, could he play! I always struggled with any instrument I tried. And thanks to my dad, I had tried a lot. And here was Doc Watson, unable to see the strings, just tearing it up. But more than his playing, his voice had a ghostly aspect to it. I realized that a number of songs were murder ballads, old songs where the person singing had killed someone, usually the person he loved. That's pretty messed up. To say nothing of misogynistic.

I always found songs that glorify violence against women to be stupid and disgusting. But these were different somehow. He didn't seem to be glorifying the violence. You could hear how haunted he felt. I almost believed that Doc Watson was singing about his own experiences, but I'm pretty sure he wasn't. At least, I hoped he wasn't.

I ended up listening to several Doc Watson records before Granny called me to dinner later that evening. I'm not saying the music put me in a better mood. I mean, with all the murder and heartbreak, how could it? I was just in a different mood. Maybe a little more thoughtful.

The next day Mr. Snead handed back the poetry appreciation essays. As he walked down the aisles, calling out names and handing back papers, I saw several people mouthing *Yes!* and punching the air. That seemed like a good sign.

Shawn got his and quickly skimmed through the comments and then looked at the last page for his grade. When he saw that I was looking over at him, he gave me a quick thumbs-up.

"Miss Talcott," said Mr. Snead, holding out my essay.

I took it and saw that there was a lot of red ink all over it. I mean, a lot.

At the top, he had written *Milan Kundera?* What the heck was that supposed to mean?

The rest of the comments were mostly corrections on my spelling and grammar. Okay, so I'm not the best speller and I have a few issues with grammar. Sue me. There were a few comments saying that I was giving the writer of the song "too much credit." It was clear that he had a problem with me writing my essay on a Lite Brite song.

At the end of the paper, Snead had written: *Setting aside all the stylistic problems with your paper, both the 'poem' and the essay seem devoid of serious content. Perhaps when the subject matter is as vapid as this pop song appears to be, one can only assume the 'analysis' will be vapid too.*

Dang!

I told you Snead hated me.

At the bottom of the last page was my grade.

D+.

8

I was devastated by my D+.

"It's not fair," I complained to Shawn, as I flopped down on the bus seat next to him. "That butthead clearly hates me."

"Well, I'm not so sure 'bout that."

"Why allow people to write on song lyrics if you are just going to be a judgmental jerk about it?"

Shawn paused. "True. But there were a lot of writing mistakes in your paper."

I was beginning to regret showing him my paper after class. Shawn had gotten an A+ for his essay on "Shady Grove," but I knew that it was well deserved. What with Shawn being a genius and all.

"He gave everyone who wrote on a Bob Dylan song good grades. It's only because I wrote on a song by an all-female punk band. Snead is just a sexist and a...uh...punkist!"

"Well, there *were* a lot of spelling and grammar errors."

"Okay, okay! I get it." I snapped.

Shawn looked out the window and then added, "I mean, how can someone who reads as much as you spell so horribly? Don't you pay attention to the words that you're reading?"

"Okay, shut it, buster," I snarled. For being such a big wuss, Shawn was flirting with danger.

Shawn shrugged. "Just sayin'. But seriously, next time, if you want help cleanin' up your writing, I'd be happy to lend a hand."

I sat, brooding for a minute. That was pretty nice of him, actually. I'd be an idiot not to get help from a genius if they were offering.

"Thanks. Maybe I will."

"No problem." Shawn waited a few moments and then looked at me with a smile. "Punkist, huh?"

"Shut up!" I laughed and pretended to punch him in the arm. Shawn flinched sideways and bonked his head on the bus window.

Served him right.

There was an official-looking envelope sitting on the kitchen table waiting for me. It was from the mayor of Beaver Dam. It was two sentences long:

```
Dear Mr. Sydney Talcott:
Thank you for your interest in the proposed
asphalt plant. There will be a public hear-
ing on the matter by the county's zoning com-
mittee on March 3rd at 5 p.m. at the county
municipal building.
```

That was all it said.

Not only was the mayor not going to do anything, the jerkface couldn't get my gender right.

Wait, March 3rd was the next day.

At dinner Grandpop agreed to drive me into town so I could attend the public hearing. Granny wanted to know what we were talking about, and when I explained about the proposed asphalt plant, she said that she wanted to go as well.

So next evening, while Mom was still working on campus, the three of us piled into the pickup truck and drove to the county offices. We wandered the empty halls until we asked a guy in a suit who was locking up his office where the zoning committee was meeting. He pointed down the hall. "Last door on the right."

When we walked in, there were two tables pushed together on one side of the room, with four people sitting behind them: three guys in ties with only one in a jacket, and a woman at the end who seemed to be taking notes. I assumed they were the zoning committee. There were chairs lined up in the rest of the room, four rows of eight chairs. But most of the chairs were empty, with only four people in the audience. All four sat in the front row, and all four were white dudes in business suits.

Everyone stopped talking and looked at us when we walked in.

"Can I help you?" asked one of the shirt-sleeved guys at the table.

I spoke up, "We're here for the zoning committee meeting."

"Oh, well, you're in the right place. Come on in."

We found seats in the back row. As Grandpop shuffled between the chairs he nodded to one of the men in the audience. "Bradley," he said.

"Mr. Avery," the man said to Grandpop. He looked over at Granny, who seemed to be doing her best to ignore him. Using my super-sleuthing skills, I deduced that he must be Bradley Winter. He was wearing a dark suit with a red tie. He seemed like he'd probably been an athlete in school but had started to go soft from aging and eating. He had a boring, immaculate haircut that accentuated the healthy dose of gray on the sides. He reeked of Slytherin. The jacketed guy at the table looked like a younger, skinnier, less gray version of him. Being such a super-sleuth, I concluded that he must be Stephen Winter.

The jacket guy cleared his throat. "Yes, so if we can get back to our agenda, we were just wrapping up the opening presentation on the proposal to construct the asphalt plant on Laurel Ridge Road. Have you anything else to add, Mr. Sampson?"

One of the men in the front row stood up. "Thank you, Mr. Winter. No, I think we've covered all the reasons why this plant is necessary. But to reiterate," he said, turning slightly to face the three of us sitting behind him. "The development that is taking place around Laurel Ridge has increased the demand for asphalt. Creating a new asphalt plant on this side of the county will make this development, particularly the necessary road construction, more efficient and cheaper. Plus, it will make Beaver Dam safer, so that we decrease the number of heavy trucks carrying asphalt from across the county for these projects. Finally, it will boost the economy of Beaver Dam, both indirectly through the development along Laurel Ridge, but also directly, as the asphalt plant will provide almost half a dozen new jobs for the county. As the representative of HD Dunkirk Industries, we are pleased to partner with Beaver Dam on this journey of growth and expansion."

"Oh, puh-lease," Granny said under her breath. I saw Grandpop nudge her gently.

"Thank you, Mr. Sampson." Stephen Winter then turned to his brother. "We will now hear from Mr. Bradley Winter, the current owner of this land."

"Thank you, Stephen," Bradley Winter said, also standing. Even though there were only a handful of people in the room, most of whom he seemed to know, his voice was loud and pompous. "My legal counsel is here as well, but we've nothing to add. As the zoning committee knows, our sale of this land is contingent on HD Dunkirk Industries receiving authorization to build this much-needed plant. We, too, are happy to be working with such an esteemed business to grow and strengthen the wonderful town of Beaver Dam and the surrounding environs. Thank you all very much."

As he sat back down, Granny muttered, "Bozo." Grandpop nudged her, a little harder this time.

"Thank you, Mr. Winter. And now we will open the floor to comments from the public on this proposal. The floor is now open." All three men of the zoning committee looked to Grandpop, Granny, and me. After a moment, the lady taking notes also looked up at us. I'm not sure what I thought would happen. In my mind, I thought the room would have been packed with people wanting to talk about the proposed asphalt plant. In fact, I assumed the room would have been bigger. But it was smaller than any of my school classrooms. There was nobody here. Didn't anybody care about the asphalt plant?

I don't know why, but I raised my hand. I figured it was what Joan Jett would have done.

"Yes, the floor recognizes...um, could you stand and state your name, please?"

I stood up, my cheeks flush and my knees feeling a little wobbly. "Um, my name is Sydney Talcott." At that, Bradley Winter turned fully around in his seat to get a good look at me. I wondered if Bethany had mentioned me. If so, I wondered what she had said. I'm sure it wasn't good.

"Um, yes. I just wanted to speak against this proposed asphalt plant." Now everyone in the front row turned around to look at me. Feeling everyone's eyes on me, I continued. "I'm a student at Beaver Dam Middle School which is right up the road from where they want to build this asphalt plant. I've been doing research, and I've found out that asphalt plants are dangerous to the people and the environment around them. They produce toxic fumes that are known to cause cancer. And when they are in places where there is lots of fog, like here in Beaver Dam, they are even more dangerous because the toxins get caught in the fog. This plant is bad for Beaver Dam, especially since there is a school right down the road." Looking back and forth between the two Mr. Winters, I added, "Surely you don't want the children of Beaver Dam, especially your own children, to get cancer. Thank you."

Granny whispered, "Nicely said, Sydney," as I sat down.

I don't know what I thought would happen next. Maybe for the zoning committee to start questioning the representatives from HD Dunkirk about the cancer-causing aspects of asphalt production.

But I didn't expect to get laughed at. Which is exactly what happened.

The two representatives from HD Dunkirk both started chuckling. After a second, Stephen Winter joined in. "Well, thank you for that, young lady," he said in a highly patronizing tone. "I think your research might be mistaken. Asphalt plants are completely safe. And HD Dunkirk Industries is already scheduled to submit an environmental impact report on the site in," he looked down at the papers in front of him, "...um...in six weeks. At which point, we will reconvene for final approval of this project. Unless there are no further comments—"

"Now hold on a second there," I heard Grandpop say. Granny looked stunned. Grandpop rarely spoke in public. "Maybe I heard you wrong there, Stephen, but did you just say that HD Dunkirk Industries is writin' their own environmental impact report?"

"Um, yes, Mr. Avery. It is the zoning committee's prerogative to delegate the submission of an environmental impact report to a third-party. Doing so will save the county a tremendous amount of money."

"But HD Dunkirk ain't no third party," Grandpop said slowly, as if talking to a toddler. "They're the ones doin' the building. Of course they aren't gonna say what they're about to do is gonna cause any harm."

The representatives from HD Dunkirk Industries both started to speak, but Mr. Winter signaled to them to stay quiet. The other two members of the zoning committee shifted uncomfortably in their seats. "Mr. Avery, HD Dunkirk Industries operates their own office that does reports like this all the time. Surely you aren't suggesting anything untoward is taking place."

I'm not sure what *untoward* means. But if it is what Holden Caulfield would call you-know-what, then I'm pretty sure that was exactly what Grandpop was implying.

Grandpop shook his head slowly. "That's like askin' the fox to guard the hen-house. That ain't right."

"As I said, Mr. Avery, it is in the zoning committee's prerogative to delegate this expensive work, and our associates are more than qualified to provide a fair and balanced report on the environmental impact of this much-needed plant."

Grandpop rose to his feet, staring at each of the men at the table. "That ain't right. You boys know that ain't right." He glanced down at Granny and me. "C'mon, it's best we get out of here."

As she rose, Granny turned to the men at the front of the room, shooting daggers from her eyes, and, in a voice dripping with razor-sharp sarcasm, said, "Well, bless your hearts. Just bless your hearts." I had been in the South long enough to know that she meant the exact opposite.

As we left the room, Stephen Winter was saying something about upcoming business. When I glanced back, they had all turned back to their conversation. Except Bradley Winter, who was still turned around in his seat staring right at me.

Creepy.

As we drove back home, Grandpop kept quiet, but you could tell he was deep in thought. He was driving even more carefully than usual, given the thick fog that had rolled in.

Granny, on the other hand, did not hold her tongue. As soon as we were in the pickup truck, she began a steady stream of abuse. She had strong opinions about everybody who had been in that room, and none of them positive.

"It's just typical that those clowns would want to sacrifice the beauty of the mountains in order to line their pockets. They won't be happy until they've got ugly box stores like that Harris Teeter all over these mountains. I swear, all they do is worship at the Church of the Almighty Dollar."

It went on like that for several minutes.

Then she looked at me. "Is that true what you said about asphalt plants, Sydney?"

"Uh, yeah. I read that long-term asphalt fumes can cause cancer. And I read a report that says in locations with heavy fog, like around here," I gestured out the front window to the dense fog that we were passing through, "the toxins stay in the atmosphere longer than usual."

"Where'd you read that stuff?"

"I did some research at school during my lunch period."

"You did that on your own? Not for a class or nothin'?"

"Nope," I said, deciding it best not mention Ms. Yancey's help. "I wanted to find out more about asphalt plants after seeing the sign on my bus ride. It didn't seem right to be building one so close to where kids are going to school."

"It ain't right," Granny said, patting my leg and turning back toward the road. "And you did real good back there, sweetie. Real good."

In the darkness I could see Grandpop nodding in agreement. I appreciated their praise, but it didn't change my feelings of helplessness. The zoning committee didn't care and they were clearly in cahoots with HD Dunkirk Industries. I mean, Grandpop was right, how crazy was it to let HD Dunkirk Industries write its own environmental impact report?

"I didn't even mention HD Dunkirk's horrible history," I added.

Granny turned to look at me again. "What do you mean?"

I briefly told them what I had learnedt about HD Dunkirk, the accidents they had caused and the lawsuits against them.

"It figures them Winter boys would be neck deep with dirty folks like that. I always knew them boys were no good."

"Is it true that Mom and Bradley Winter used to date?"

Granny laughed mirthlessly while shaking her head. "Oh, lordy, yes. They were thick as thieves, those two. All the way back in elementary school they were best buddies. Then they started getting romantic-like in high school. But by then Bradley was starting to get more and more like his daddy. He'd been a decent enough kid but then his daddy started bringing him into the family business. Bradley became more concerned with the type of car he was drivin' and the brand of clothes he was wearin'. He followed your momma off to college but dropped out after one year. Think he was a little homesick, if you ask me. Missed being such a big fish in a small bowl. So he came back to Beaver Dam and took over all of his daddy's businesses. But he would visit your momma every weekend." Granny paused for a second. "I don't think he ever forgave her for runnin' off with your daddy. Your momma would never admit it, but I think she took up with your daddy in order to escape from Bradley."

Granny continued on, but I kind of tuned her out. I kept thinking about Mom dating Bethany's dad, and what that would have meant.

I guess I had a lot to be thankful for.

A couple of days later, two pieces of mail came. One for me and one about me.

The one for me was from Dani.

Hey, Sydney! Thanks so much for your awesome letter. First let me just say that it is so cool that you wrote an essay about a Lite Brite song. I hope it was OK, but I told the band about it at practice a few days ago. They were all super stoked. And I'm glad you wrote on the "Unbearable Lightness of Being a Girl." I loved Milan Kundera when I first read him [Wait, it's a writer-dude? Okay, clearly I need to find out who this is!] but I hated his misogyny, which is characteristic of so many of his books. I can't read his stuff anymore, but he helped inspire that song and it is one of my favorites of our older songs. I sure hope you got a good grade! I'm glad things in Beaver Dam are getting better. I am sure you miss Rochester and your friends there, but it sounds like Shawn and Rita are pretty cool! Yay for friends! That also sounds crazy about that asphalt plant. Good for you for doing some research [Maybe I should have done a bit of research before I wrote that paper for Snead]. So many people just accept what is going on around them, without asking questions or looking closer into what is happening or why. We've been working on getting together a group of folks here to try to deal with the hunger problem in our neighborhood. As someone who bakes for a profession—and likes to eat!—hunger is an important issue for me. I'm glad you are finding issues that are important to you. Keep me posted on how you are doing with that fight. It sounds like a really important issue—affecting the environment and people's health! I talked with your brother the other day. If your ears were burning it was because we were talking about you! All good stuff, I promise. We're finishing up the new album and starting to think about going on tour in the spring. Because we all have jobs, summer tours are a bit more of a challenge. So we're hoping to get something together for late spring. OK, gotta run. Write me back and let me know what's shaking with you!

xoxo DANI.

Again, there was a little drawing of Dani at the end of the page. In one hand was a guitar and the other was what looked like a piece of cake. Next to it she'd written "My two loves = music and food!"

I went up to my room, put on some music, and wrote her back. I told her that my essay didn't win any awards (I didn't tell her the exact grade!) but that it was mostly my fault because of my horrible spelling and grammar. I didn't admit to not knowing who Milan Kundera was, but I did mention that Shawn had offered to proofread future papers. I also told her about the zoning committee meeting. I hadn't planned on giving her all the details, but once I started, I couldn't stop. I told her how bummed I was because it seemed like there was nothing I could do. The zoning committee, the Winters, and Dunkirk Industries all seemed to be working together. And judging from the complete lack of attendance, nobody seemed to care. Though, thinking about Rita's response, I wondered if some people were too scared to say anything for fear of angering the Winter family.

I apologized to Dani for getting all depressed, and I ended the letter by talking about discovering a cool record store in Franklin where the clerk had recognized my Lite Brite shirt. I told her about The Ward Cleavers and about their song "Mountain Laurel."

I had just finished when I heard Granny calling me.

And that's when I found out that the other letter was about me.

Granny was standing in the kitchen with a letter in her hand. "Sydney, do you know what this is?"

At first I didn't realize that she was so angry, which is why I said something stupid like, "I believe it is what the kids these days call a l-e-t-t-e-r."

"It's a midterm report from your school."

Uh-oh. Her attitude let me know I had reason to be concerned. "I'm doing fine in almost all of my classes," I said. Which was true. I was doing better than fine in everything but English.

"There is this little matter of a D+ average in English. That certainly isn't 'doing fine,' is it?"

"No, ma'am. But Mr. Snead hates me, he really does."

"Come off it, Sydney."

"It's true. I'm doing fine in all my other classes, aren't I?"

"Well, yes." She hesitated. "But there's also a note that your social studies teacher sent you to the principal's office for an altercation with another student. What's that about?"

"Now, that was *not* my fault!"

"It seems like nothin' is your fault," Granny shot back. "Now, I know this transition has been hard on you. But failin' classes and gettin' into trouble is simply unacceptable, young lady."

I knew this was not argument I was going to win, but I wasn't about to surrender yet. "Listen, Granny. The altercation in social studies was caused by Bethany Winter. She's been bullying me, but I was the one who got in trouble."

At the sound of Bethany's name, Granny's anger seemed to falter a bit. Her eyes narrowed on me. "What do you mean 'bullying'?"

"Well, it's not like she's beating me up or anything, but Bethany and her friends are always picking on me. That morning they stole my book and were taunting me. I finally snapped and pushed back, and that's when Mrs. Critcher walked in. But she only saw what I did."

Granny kept staring at me dubiously, but I could see she was processing this information.

"I was provoked by Bethany Winter, I promise. She started it. But it won't happen again. She's not worth getting in trouble over."

"That's certainly true. None of them Winters are," said

Granny after a second. Then she held up the midterm report, "But what about this D+ in English?"

"Okay, there is room for improvement, I admit. But for what it is worth, I have already made plans to get help in that class."

"So you have spoken with your teacher about your grade?"

"No way! Seriously, Mr. Snead hates me. But my friend Shawn is a certifiable genius and he agreed to help me out with my writing on future assignments. Working on my spelling and grammar and that kind of thing."

"Hmm. Well, I want you to talk with this Mr. Snead to see what *he* thinks you can be doing to improve your grade."

"But Granny…"

"No *buts*, Sydney. I want you to talk to your teacher this week about your grade. Or else. Do you understand me?"

"Yes, ma'am," I conceded.

"And no trips to Franklin for the time being," she added.

"What? But I was hoping to go this weekend to visit the record store!"

"Nope, not this weekend, you aren't. And of course I'll have to share this report with your momma when she gets home, and we'll see what she has to say about it as well."

It turns out that Granny was way more upset by the midterm report than Mom was. Mom got home late that evening and I was already in bed when she knocked on the door of my room and came in. I had been reading when I heard her walking up the stairs and had quickly turned off the light.

"Sydney, I know you're still awake."

"Just barely," I lied.

She lay down on the bed next to me, staring at the ceiling. When she spoke, her voice was heavy and tired, thick like porridge. "Granny shared your midterm report with me."

"Pretty good, huh? A and B averages in all classes but one."

"Yeah, it's that one I'm concerned about. You have a D+ in English, Sydney. You know I'm not going to tolerate that."

"I know, but I'm getting help to improve my grade."

"Granny said that she wants you to talk to the teacher tomorrow. I think that's a good idea. I hated it when she used to make me do that, but it always paid off."

"Are you admitting not getting perfect grades when you were a student?" I teased, trying to use humor to defuse any anger.

When Mom chuckled, even her laugh sounded tired. "We're talking about you, not me. But, yeah, I had a few missteps. Thankfully Granny was there to straighten me out." She yawned an epically long yawn. "And what's this about getting in a fight?"

"There was no fight. Just Bethany Winter picking on me, but the teacher only came in when I was defending myself."

"I know it's tough being the new kid, sweetpea. But try to keep your head above the fray."

We lay there for a minute in the darkness of my room. I remembered that, once upon a time, this had been Mom's room. She'd lived in this room until she'd gone off to college. That got me thinking about her and Bradley Winter.

"Were you really engaged to Bethany Winter's dad? What was that all about?"

I thought she was thinking about how to answer, but she never gave one.

Not unless you consider snoring to be an answer.

9

When I admitted to Granny the following afternoon that I hadn't spoken to Mr. Snead yet, she kinda went off on me. I tried to explain that I hadn't even had English that day, but that didn't matter to her. Not wanting to experience her wrath again, I approached Mr. Snead at the end of our English class the next day.

As the other students were piling out of the class, I walked up to his desk. He was sitting down, going through one of the side drawers, trying to find something.

"Um, excuse me, Mr. Snead."

I swear he grimaced when he looked up and saw it was me.

"Yes, Miss Talcott. Can I help you?"

"Well, it's about the midterm report that went home this week."

He returned to his search of the drawer. "Mm-hmm," he said distractedly.

"Well, it's just that I was a little concerned about my grade for this class."

"I imagine you would be. You seem to be performing quite poorly so far."

"That's the thing. I don't think you're being fair to me."

He slammed the drawer shut. Okay, maybe he just closed it. But it sure felt like he was slamming it shut. "Fair? And how exactly am I being unfair to you, Miss Talcott?"

"Well," I said, feeling a little unsure of myself. "I thought the poetry appreciation paper I did was pretty good."

"Ah, yes, your analysis of the pop song. Did you happen to read over your paper before you handed it in, Miss Talcott?"

"Um…"

"Exactly. There is a thing called proofreading. I suggest you get familiar with it. Moreover," he continued in a patronizing voice, "you may want to be more discerning on what you choose to write."

"See! I knew I got the bad grade because you didn't like my taste in music!" I shouted indignantly.

Mr. Snead sighed so heavily that a paper on his desk shook. He looked down at it with surprise and picked it up. I guessed that was what he had been looking for in the side drawers of his desk. "I can assure you, Miss Talcott, that I could care less about whatever type of garbage you choose to cram into your ears. You can pick your own poison. But don't try to pass that trifle off as literature. In order to analyze poetry, one must begin with a poem. Not something made up entirely of la-la-las."

I was angry. There were no *la-la-las* in that Lite Brite song. Sure, there were plenty in their other songs. But not in that one.

Mr. Snead stood up from his desk with the newly discovered paper in his hands. "Meanwhile, I suggest you purchase a good dictionary to help you with your writing."

Okay, that stung. Mostly because I knew there was some truth behind it.

"Well, Shawn has agreed to help me with that in the future."

Snead narrowed his eyes at me. "Shawn? Shawn Tucker?"

"Yeah, Shawn's a friend of mine. He said he'd help me with my writing." Suddenly I felt a panic. Maybe that wasn't allowed at this school. "I mean, if that's okay."

"That's perfectly fine. I'm sure the help will do you a world of good." He paused for a second before adding, "It seems your choice in friends is better than your choice in music."

Before I could respond, he continued, "Now, if you will excuse me, Miss Talcott. I have copies to make for my next class."

And he walked out.

On the bus ride home, I noticed several big trucks parked inside the fence of the proposed asphalt plant. A couple of diggers and at least two dump trucks lurked by the gate, but I didn't see anyone walking around.

"That's weird," I said to Shawn, looking back as the bus drove past.

"What is?"

He'd been talking about a new science fiction series he had started, N.K. Jemisin's *The Fifth Season* trilogy. I wasn't a big fan of the genre, and Shawn was trying to convince me that this series was better than typical science fiction.

"There's heavy equipment parked over there."

Shawn was confused for a second, until he realized I wasn't talking about the *Fifth Season* series, but what was happening in the real world.

"Where? Oh, at the asphalt plant. I guess they are startin' to prepare the site."

"But the proposal hasn't been approved yet. The company still has to turn in an environmental impact report."

Shawn shrugged his shoulders and resumed his promotion of N.K. Jemisin's brilliance.

Later, when I got home, Granny seemed satisfied when I told her that I'd talked to Snead and had even gotten his approval for having Shawn proofread my future papers.

"That's good. But if your grade continues to be so dismal, I'll start goin' over your work as well."

"There won't be any need for that," I responded quickly. If I thought Mr. Snead didn't like my music taste, I knew Granny straight up hated it. She would have blown a gasket if she knew I had written an English paper on a Lite Brite song. She'd have argued I deserved an F—not a D+.

"Oh, and you got a letter today, sweetpea," Granny said, pulling out a pink envelope from her apron pocket.

It was from Kris. When the heck did Kris start using pink envelopes?

A month or two before, I would have been ecstatic to receive a letter from Kris, even one on pink stationery. Now I was a little apprehensive. I hadn't heard from her in almost two weeks. When she had written, she never asked questions about my life. It was all about her life with the twins and how cute "Stu" was.

This letter was more of the same. But worse.

It seemed that she and Stu were now officially "dating," whatever the heck that meant.

Barf.

Later that afternoon, Granny asked me if I wanted to go with her to Harris Teeter for groceries. I still had some homework to do but wasn't much in the mood after getting that letter from Kris.

Granny and I had a routine when we went grocery shopping. I would grab my own cart and fill it with all the breakfast, lunch, and snack foods that I wanted, and then meet her at the checkout where she'd pay for both her and my carts.

Since as long as I can remember, I had always made my own breakfast in the morning (sometimes with Joey's help) and packed my own school lunches. Back in Rochester, Mom and Dad had taken turns cooking dinner. Then it was just Mom and frozen dinners. But here Granny cooked dinner most of the time.

As long as I had some fruits and vegetables mixed in with my snacks, Granny was pretty much fine with whatever I got. I didn't go in for junk food anyway, but I will admit to having a slight addiction to yogurt-covered raisins and chocolate chip cookies.

The Harris Teeter was still shiny and new, with wide aisles, unlike the grocery stores that we'd go to back in Rochester. Those seemed packed tighter and definitely had more people in them. I grabbed two boxes of cereal. One was an expensive granola with pecans and the other a generic box of raisin bran. I liked to mix my cereals together in the morning and believed that the fancy granola raised the quality of whatever I mixed it with. I turned into the next aisle and almost ran right into a man pushing his cart.

"Oh, sorry," I said. Then I looked up and froze.

It was Bradley Winter.

He scowled at me for a few seconds. There was no one else in the aisle and I swear the temperature in the store dropped a few degrees. If I hadn't known better, I would have sworn we were standing in the ice cream section.

"Well, well. It's Sydney, isn't it?" His voice had an icy pierce to it.

"Um, yeah. Sydney Talcott."

"Talcott, that's right," he said, appraising me. "The girl from New York who likes sticking her nose into people's business. And I understand you've been bullying my child at school."

I was totally confused, which is why I said, "Your kid's being bullied? That's horrible." I thought for a second before adding, "Is that Bethany's sister or brother? I thought Bethany was an only child."

"Very funny. I am talking about Bethany. She tells me you've been threatening her and calling her names."

"What? That's crazy! Bethany is the one who has been harassing me!"

"She said you were sent to the principal's office for swearing at her and physically assaulting her. Isn't that right?"

"No! Well, not exactly…" I said, flustered.

He moved his cart around until he had pulled up next to me. Leaning toward me, I could smell his cologne. It was probably expensive, but it was definitely stinky. "Let me make this perfectly clear, little lady. You don't mess with me, with my business, or my family." He leaned in a bit closer, right in my face, the smell of his cologne making my eyes water. "Especially not my family."

A young woman with a little kid sitting in an overflowing shopping cart rounded the corner at the far end of the aisle. Bradley Winter straightened up, looked me over, and started to walk away.

I was a mishmash of emotions. Confusion, some repulsion from his cologne, mostly fear. But now joined by a surge of anger. Did this guy just threaten me? I don't like being threatened by big, evil dudes. Especially when they call me "little lady." I didn't need to think what Joan Jett might do.

I called after him, "Excuse me, Mr. Winter?"

He turned slowly, his eyes narrowing on me. "Yes?"

"What are all those trucks and diggers doing on that land? You don't have permission to build that asphalt plant yet. I hope you aren't getting ahead of yourself or breaking any laws."

He glowered at me for a few seconds. I think he was trying to be intimidating. Truth be told, he was doing a pretty good job of it. "Don't you worry yourself with that, little lady. The asphalt plant will get built, you can mark my words."

"We'll see," I said, trying to be as cool as possible. "But one more thing."

He arched an eyebrow at me, as if he was too annoyed to respond.

"Have you always been such a jerkface? If so, I can see why my mom dumped your ugly butt. Also, your cologne smells like monkey barf."

I turned on my heel and pushed my cart past the mom with her kid, who was trying to act like she hadn't just heard me call the most powerful man in Beaver Dam an ugly stinky-butt.

Man, I hate being called "little lady."

At lunch the next day, I told Shawn and Rita about the Great

Harris Teeter Showdown with Bradley Winter. Shawn was impressed, if not a little disbelieving.

"You said that to his face?"

"Yeppers," I said proudly.

"And you used your actual vocal cords. Not an internal voice?"

"Um, yes."

"And he heard you? You weren't, like, talkin' under your breath?"

I laughed. "Oh yeah, he heard me. He was as close to me as you are now and I was using a voice louder than this. Because, you know, Ms. Yancey wasn't around to hush me."

"And what'd he do?"

"I don't know. I didn't stick around to find out."

"Dang. That's impressive. Remind me not to get on your bad side...or to wear cologne around you," Shawn added.

"Yeah, please don't do either of those things."

I took out one of the apples I had bought the afternoon before and polished it with my Jabber T-shirt. "But I've been thinking," I continued, taking a bite out of the apple. "We should write a letter to the paper or something to complain about the asphalt plant. You know, expose the connections between the Winters and HD Dunkirk."

"Whoa, whoa. What are you talking about, Sydney?" Rita asked. She'd been quiet while I was telling my story, but now she looked a little scared.

"I'm talking about making people aware of what's going on. And hopefully of stopping it."

"But we're just kids. Who's gonna care what we say?"

"We're students at the school near the proposed plant. People are certain to listen to us. We could even see if other students want to sign the letter."

"I don't know about that, Sydney," Shawn said, with a concerned look on his face. "I'm not sure many people would want to sign a letter like that."

"Why not?" I was getting annoyed. "Don't they care about the environment? About not getting cancer? About the crooked dealings between the Winter family and Dunkirk Industries?"

"Sydney, are you sure this isn't just about you trying to get even with Bethany and her dad?" Rita responded.

"What? Are you kidding? This is much bigger than a petty personal grudge. They are gonna destroy the environment and give us all cancer!"

Ms. Yancey's head popped out around a corner, her face stern. "Shhhhh!"

"C'mon," I whispered. "Don't you care about this asphalt plant? What are you scared of?"

Rita glowered at me but didn't respond.

Shawn spoke softly and slowly, trying to calm things down. "Of course we care, Sydney. And we know this is important to you. It's just I'm not sure other folk will feel the same way. They don't have the information that you have."

"Which is why we need to spread the word," I said, my voice rising again. "If I write the letter, will you guys sign it with me?"

Rita looked at me, and then looked away. "I don't think I can do that, Sydney."

"Oh, come on!" I was getting angry and I didn't care if Ms. Yancey shushed me. Rita and Shawn were my friends. They were supposed to support me. "Quit being such a chicken!"

Rita looked at me angrily, but didn't respond.

I continued, pushing harder, "I thought you were my friends."

"We *are* your friends," interrupted Shawn. "It's just that—"

"Just nothing! If my *real* friends were here, they'd support me. If Kris were here, she'd help me."

"Well, I'm not Kris!" Rita shot back.

"Clearly!" I said, before I could stop myself.

As Ms. Yancey came around the corner to hush us, Rita

grabbed her backpack and stormed out of the library. I apologized to Ms. Yancey, who shot me a look before disappearing behind a bookshelf. I was still angry, but I had the feeling that I might have gone too far. Why had I even mentioned Kris? The fact was that Kris was no longer a friend I could count on. But at least she would have understood why this was important. Why wasn't Rita more like Kris? Or at least like Kris used to be?

Shawn had retreated behind a book and was giving off a vibe that he didn't want to talk to me anymore.

Fine. I didn't want to talk to him either.

On the bus ride home, I made a point of sitting several rows behind Shawn. I was still angry and didn't want to talk to him. But I had to sit behind Philip Greene, who was loudly bragging about his new hunting rifle.

When I got home, there were no letters waiting for me. Nothing from Kris. Nothing from Dani. Still grounded and unable to visit the record store in Franklin, I was prepared to spend all weekend feeling sorry for myself. And I had good reason to. School sucked. My teachers sucked. Bethany sucked. Bethany's dad sucked. My friends sucked.

Oh my God, I sounded like Holden Caulfield.

10

On Monday, I decided to eat my lunch in the cafeteria. I just wasn't up to dealing with my so-called friends.

Instead, I had to deal with my enemies.

I sat by myself at the end of a long table, feeling sorry for myself. I had just sipped my yogurt drink, when suddenly I was shoved forward. Someone had intentionally bumped into me, timing it perfectly so the drink splashed down the front of my Lite Brite shirt.

I heard a familiar grating voice from behind me. "Oh, look, Vicious Sydney has a drinkin' problem!" A chorus of cackling responded on cue.

"Watch that big butt of yours, Bethany." I didn't bother turning around. I picked up my napkin and started wiping the yogurt drink off my shirt. But most of it was already sinking in. Dang it. This was my favorite shirt. And it'd probably smell like sour milk from now on.

I had already been feeling lonely and super sad. Having my favorite shirt ruined was almost too much. I fought hard to keep the tears back. But I really wanted to cry. I wanted to run out of the school. I wanted to be back in my bedroom. My real bedroom. The one in Rochester. I wanted to curl up on my real bed under a big pile of blankets, and just cry myself to sleep.

Bethany jostled me again. This time much harder.

"Cut it out, fart-knocker, I'm warning you." My voice cracked slightly.

"Ah, is Vicious Sydney sittin' all by herself? Did no one wanna sit with you? How sad! But I can't say I blame 'em. You smell like spilt milk."

I looked around. Most people were engrossed in their own thing, but a few students were staring at Bethany and me. But not a single adult was paying any attention to us. Some even seemed to be intentionally ignoring us. And Bethany's friends—with the twins dressed in matching baby blue sweaters and khakis—seemed positioned to block their view.

I knew Bethany would continue picking on me if I tried to keep eating, so I shoved the remaining bits of my lunch back into my lunch bag. I didn't have much of an appetite anyway.

"Ah, don't tell me you're all finished with your lunch," taunted Bethany. "It's probably just as well. I didn't want to mention it, but your butt has been gettin' pretty big." The dumb bunny club giggled and snorted.

I picked up my lunch bag and backpack, stood up and turned to face Bethany. She was only inches away from my face. I had never noticed how green her eyes were. They contrasted sharply with that blonde hair of hers.

I had read somewhere that only two percent of the world's population had blonde hair. I'm sure it was a lot higher if you counted all the fake blondes, like Bethany's bleach bunnies standing behind her.

But Bethany looked like the real thing.

I was focusing my thoughts on hair color in order to keep myself calm and not start crying. Or punching. There was a good chance I might start punching. Instead, I thought about what Joan Jett might do.

She'd probably start punching. Maybe not the best idea.

"Quit looking at my butt, you creep. And I just lost my appetite. I'm sure you have that effect on most people."

She curled her lip at me. "Looks like your loser friends finally kicked you to the curb. Why don't you take the hint and crawl back to New York where you belong?"

"At least back there, they arrest corrupt scumbags like your daddy."

Bethany leaned closer and whispered, "My daddy'll bury you and your family of losers."

I looked at her and, channeling my internal non-punching Joan Jett, smiled. "Please. My family has a long history of putting the Winters in their place."

Bethany looked confused for a second. She hadn't been expecting that for a response.

"Oh, didn't your daddy tell you how my mom dumped his sorry butt back in the day? He was a loser then and he's a loser now." I pushed past her to leave the cafeteria, adding, "Just like you."

The Clueless Chorus hadn't been able to hear the last few things we'd been saying, so they were looking at Bethany and me with confused expressions. As I passed, I said to the twins, "I know you all look the same, but you don't have to dress the same. Be an individual, get a personality."

They stared blankly at me.

Oh well, I tried.

As I moved past them I heard Bethany snarl, "Watch your step, Talcott."

I started heading over to the library to tell Rita and Shawn all about this exchange, but then I stopped myself. I was still mad at them and I didn't want to deal with their disapproval. I decided to go outside to the parking lot for the rest of lunch.

Technically, I don't think students were allowed to be outside the building during school hours. But I didn't care. I stood there, just to the side of the back door, bouncing on my feet to stay warm. The strength that my internal Joan Jett had given me faded away, leaving me even more lonely, shaken, and sad than I had been before Bethany started picking on me. There were cold droplets of water running down my face, so I may or may not have been crying.

I'd been there for a few minutes when the door opened and a teacher walked out. I was standing off to the side, so he didn't notice me at first. It was a guy wearing a long overcoat and carrying what looked like a shrunken guitar case. He walked to the parking lot, opened the trunk of a small, beat-up little car, and gently lowered the instrument case into it.

After he closed the trunk and turned around, I saw that it was Mr. Snead. Great. Of all the teachers to catch me outside crying, it had to be Snead.

I thought about jumping behind a big bush, but there were none nearby. Plus, I saw him straighten up a little as he walked back, so I knew he had already seen me. I'm pretty sure he knew it was me because, let's admit it, nobody at this school has my excellent fashion sense.

"Miss Talcott, what do you think you are doing outside the school building?"

I didn't want him knowing I had been crying, so I tried to casually wipe my face. "Just getting some fresh air, you know. It gets a little claustrophobic in there."

He paused in front of me. I kept my face down. I didn't want to look him in the eyes, especially because I feared I might start crying for real.

"Students aren't allowed outside without authorization."

"I know. I was just going back in." I wiped my nose and tried to dry my eyes a little more.

He held the door open for me, but he didn't say anything more.

I went to the restroom and hid in a toilet stall until the bell rang.

The next day I decided that it would be too risky to eat lunch in the cafeteria. I just couldn't take any more abuse from Bethany. I feared I'd either punch her in the face or start crying. Probably both.

So I went to the library, but turned immediately to the right when I walked in, going to a far corner, getting as much distance from Rita and Shawn's table as I could.

About halfway through lunch, Ms. Yancey walked by. She stopped for a second and I could see she was thinking about saying something. I hunkered down further behind my *Ruby Redfort* book, signaling that I didn't want to talk to anyone. Taking the hint, she walked on.

The next day at lunch, I went back to that same table. But after a few minutes, Shawn came up and sat down. He took out his lunch and started reading *The Mysterious Benedict Society*. "What do you want?" I asked him after he had been there for a few minutes.

He didn't look up, but pushed his glasses up his nose a bit. "Nothin'."

"Why don't you go back and sit with Rita at your own table?" I tried to sound as snarky as possible.

"Rita's not there." He took a bite of celery and turned a page without looking up. "She hasn't been there all week."

"Really?" I said, slightly confused.

"Really. For the first few days it was blissfully quiet back there without you two." Finally he looked up, "But the silence is startin' to get to me."

"Where is Rita eating lunch? She hasn't been in the cafeteria. Or at least I haven't seen her."

"One of Rita's superpowers is invisibility. If she doesn't wanna be seen, she's good at not gettin' noticed." He started crunching on a second celery stalk.

"Huh," is all I could come up with.

"C'mon, Sydney. You're not still mad, are you?"

"Yeah, I'm still mad," I said, trying to work up my anger, but the truth was that it was nice talking to someone again. "This asphalt plant thing is important to me and you guys don't care at all."

He sighed. "We do care. And we do know that it is important to you. It's just that…We're not like you, Sydney."

"What do you mean? You guys are book nerds and outcasts just like me. I thought we were friends."

"We *are* friends. You and Rita are the only friends I have. You know that."

It was true. I'd never seen Shawn talk to another human being, except for teachers. He was rooting around in his lunch bag, and then pulled out a huge carrot. Man, that kid loved his veggies.

"It's just that you're an outcast by choice," he said, making a loud crunch as he bit into the carrot.

"What are you talking about?"

"For you, being a rebel and an outcast is a choice. It's a privilege. It's not that way for me and Rita. You're an outcast 'cause you wanna be one. But you could show up to school tomorrow with different clothes and start fittin' in, no problem. That's a privilege that Rita and I will never have. We're outcasts because of who we are. Because of the color of our skin and where we're from. That's somethin' completely different."

I started to answer, but stopped.

I didn't know what to say.

I had never thought about it that way. But it still hurt that they weren't being supportive of me. When I said that to Shawn, he responded, "If you take on the Winter family and lose, what is the worst thing that could happen to you?" Before I could answer, he pressed on. "But what would be the worst thing for Rita? She could lose her apartment. Her family and friends could get deported. Sydney, the stakes are higher for her than they are for you. Much higher."

I sighed. He was right. I hadn't thought about it that way.

"Okay, okay. I get it. Maybe I should be more sensitive."

Shawn relaxed slightly. "It would help."

"Yeah, fine. But what about you?" I dredged up a little leftover snarkiness.

He flinched slightly. "What do you mean?"

"You aren't getting deported. Why won't you fight against this asphalt plant with me?"

"Have you not met me?" Shawn smiled slightly, taking out a second carrot from his lunch bag. "I'm the biggest wuss in the school."

I waved my hand, as if brushing away his excuses. "Don't give me that, buster. You care more about these mountains than anyone else in this town. Aren't you upset about what this asphalt plant could mean to the environment?"

Shawn's face turned more serious. "Actually, yes. I do care. And I've been doin' some of my own research, and you're right 'bout all the problems it might cause."

"See!"

"And you're also right 'bout how horrible HD Dunkirk Industries is. But I just don't see what we can do. The Winter family has the county commission under their thumb and Dunkirk Industries has powerful friends in high places. I'm not sure what we can do to stop this thing from happenin'."

I had been thinking about it a lot too.

And I didn't know what to do either.

I didn't see Rita that afternoon. I waited in the hall before and after Spanish in hopes of catching her leaving her French class next door. But somehow she got past me both times. Shawn was right, invisibility was her superpower.

But it was nice to be back on good terms with Shawn.

We sat together on the bus ride home that afternoon. As we drove past the proposed asphalt plant site, the trucks and diggers were still parked with no one around, but several of the trees had been cut down and hauled off. Clearly there was work being done on the site. We talked about what we could do. But after a few minutes of coming up with nothing reasonable (though there might have been talk of getting our hands on some dynamite), we shifted our conversation to Mr. Snead's newest assignment. We had spent the last several weeks studying plays. We had read some Shakespeare (Mr. Snead had a thing for Shakespeare, but I think all middle-school English teachers are required to), as well as a few more contemporary works. The new assignment was to write either our own short play or an essay analyzing a scene from one of Shakespeare's.

"I have no idea what I am going to write," I said. 'To be honest, I'm even scared to begin. It doesn't matter if I write the play or the essay, I know he is going to hate it. And my grade in that class depends on doing well on this assignment."

"I'm sure you'll find inspiration."

"What are you going to do, the play or the essay?"

"Well, I was toyin' with the idea of doing a play based on 'Shady Grove,' but I fear that's maybe goin' to the well once too often."

"Well, he liked your paper on it, right?" I pointed out.

"Yeah, he did. He said he didn't know about the other versions of the song and that my essay had changed how he was playin' the song himself."

"What do you mean?" But then I remembered him walking out to his car with that miniature guitar case. "Does he play music?"

"Yeah, I've seen him play a few times, usually at events around town in the summer. I think he plays a bunch of instruments—banjo, fiddle, dobro, mandolin, guitar."

I tried to imagine Mr. Snead with his ugly sweater vest tearing it up on a banjo and my brain melted a little bit. It just didn't compute.

The house was silent when I walked into the kitchen. Propped up against the salt-and-pepper shakers was a note from Granny saying that Grandpop had taken her to Franklin for a doctor's appointment and that they wouldn't be back until later that afternoon. Mom was probably on campus. I was seeing her even less than usual these days.

Behind Granny's note was an envelope. I assumed it

wasn't a letter from Kris and I was right. I hadn't heard from her in ages, not since she and Stuart started "dating." Barf.

The letter was from Dani.

Hey hey, Sydney! How are things? I hope you are doing well. Things here are great. We're putting the final touches on the new album and it sounds pretty good. I think you will like it a lot. Lots of Grrrl Power songs! Hey, thanks for the tip about The Ward Cleavers. I downloaded their album and it's great. You're right, 'Mountain Laurel' is fantastic. It's my favorite song too. I love Betty's voice as much as her fiddle playing. I'm so glad you made contact with them and thanks for turning me on to their music. And thanks for keeping me posted about what is going on with the proposed asphalt plant. That is really cruddy what happened at the zoning board meeting. But not too surprising either. That is the way things work sometimes. Fortunately, we've got punk rock to show us the way, right? It was such a revelation when my punk friends here in Chicago taught me that instead of sitting around waiting for someone else to make a change, you have to do it yourself. That's why Lite Brite always books our own tours and releases our own music on our own label. And it goes beyond the music, you know. For instance, I live in a neighborhood that is what people call a 'food desert' because there are no grocery stores around here and the only two restaurants are stupid expensive. To get affordable food, people have to walk or take the bus several miles, which is just crazy, especially as most of the people in the neighborhood are poor or elderly. So some friends bought a van and drive into neighborhoods like ours to sell the food that they are buying directly from farmers out in the countryside. It's pretty cool. DIY punk culture in action. Do it yourself, or even better, do it with friends! This is what punk rock has been training us to do. I hope you can find some success in your fight. As for Lite Brite, we're still working out the late spring tour. I think Joey is going to get us a show in Buffalo. I'll let you know if we're coming anyplace close to you. It'd be so much fun to hang out with you in person!

xoxo DANI

At the bottom of the page she had drawn herself in a Rosie the Riveter pose with the speech bubble saying "We can do it!"

That night, I had a hard time falling asleep.

All I could think about was how I was going to fight the asphalt plant.

With punk rock.

11

Rita wasn't at lunch and Shawn said he hadn't seen her all day. I guess she was still sulking. Fine, whatever. But as we ate our lunch, I told Shawn about Dani's letter.

"Sorry, Sydney." He pushed his glasses up his nose. "Maybe I'm missin' something, but how is punk gonna stop an asphalt plant? Are we supposed to start a band?"

"Well, that'd be cool if we could play any instruments."

"Excuse me," he said indignantly, pulling a sandwich out of his lunch bag. "I'll have you know that I'm an excellent fiddle player."

"Really?" I had already had the earlier shock of imagining Mr. Snead playing banjo. Now I had a vision of Shawn playing fiddle on top of a haystack. I shook my head, trying to get the distracting image out of my mind. "Never mind. You're missing the point. Music won't stop the asphalt plant, but punk can."

"How's that?" He looked confused.

"Punk isn't just about making music. It's also about living a DIY life."

"What the what?" He'd been holding his sandwich in his hand, but still hadn't taken a bite as he tried to wrap his head around what I was saying.

"DIY. Do-it-yourself. Punk isn't just about raging against the machine and pointing out all the bad things in society. It's about creating solutions through personal empowerment," I said, warming up to the topic. Once I started down the path of promoting punk culture, I knew from experience that I could get carried away.

"It's about transforming yourself from being a passive

consumer into an active producer. Punks make their own music, make their own clothes, release their own music. But not in a 'turn-on, drop-out' hippie kinda way. Punks fight for social justice. But instead of asking the powers-that-be to make things better, punks do it themselves, finding their own solutions."

"Um, okay. But I still don't see how that relates here."

"Well, what are the two challenges facing us?"

"HD Dunkirk Industries and the Winter family," Shawn responded immediately.

"Yeah, okay. That's not exactly the answer I was going for." I felt frustrated that I wasn't being as clear as I wanted to be. Sometimes I wish I could just do a mind-meld with people so that they could understand exactly what I was trying to say. "I meant the challenges about getting people involved with the asphalt plant."

"Well, I don't think most people know about it," Shawn said. "None of my family did when I was talkin' 'bout it this weekend."

"Exactly! And many of those who do know are too scared of the Winter family to do anything about it. They feel powerless."

I glanced around to see if Ms. Yancey was nearby. She wasn't. I was pretty sure she belonged to that group. In addition to researching Dunkirk Industries, she had encouraged me to look into whoever owned that land, so she clearly knew what was going on. But for whatever reason, she didn't seem to be doing anything about it.

"So our two biggest challenges are ignorance and powerlessness. If there is one thing punk has taught me is that the second one is largely an illusion."

"Um, I'm pretty sure some people have more power than others," Shawn said.

"No doubt! But just because someone has more power than you doesn't make you powerless. We all have power in some way. But let's focus on the first challenge: letting people know what is going on."

"And how are we gonna do that?"

"Lite Brite has a song called 'Instrument' where Dani sings 'Your voice is your instrument.' So we're gonna use our voices. We're going to give people information. We're gonna spread the word."

"How? By writin' letters to the editor? Or puttin' advertisements in the newspaper? That costs money and they probably won't print them anyway."

"We do it ourselves, punk-rock style," I said, taking out a piece of paper from my notebook to make a list. "We can make posters and put them around town. We can make our own zines."

"Our own what?" Amazingly, the sandwich was still un-eaten in his hand, so I knew I had his complete attention.

"Zines. They are handmade little magazines."

I dug around my backpack and pulled out the battered copy of *Rochester Skate City* I had been carrying around for weeks. I explained how my old friends and I had made it about skateboarding in Rochester.

"We can make a zine like that one. We can write stories about the asphalt plant, talk about the threats to the environment, and make people aware of HD Dunkirk's accidents and lawsuits. We can photocopy it ourselves, staple the pages together, and then pass them out around town. We become our own media."

Shawn flipped through the zine for a minute.

"Okay, I know what my job is gonna be." Shawn smiled before finally taking a bite of his sandwich.

"What?"

"Fixin' all of your spellin' mistakes."

"Deal!"

We spent the rest of the lunch break drafting out what we

wanted to put in the zine. I wanted to write an opening essay about what I had learned about asphalt production, especially about the environmental concerns. We needed something about HD Dunkirk Industries. Shawn had the great idea of just listing the main headlines and opening paragraphs from some of the news articles I had found. If we just put those together, with a link to each article, it would be pretty powerful.

I offered to write a short piece about what had happened at the zoning committee meeting.

In addition to being the proofreader, Shawn volunteered to write a piece on the history of the Laurel Ridge region, since he knew so much about the area.

"How are we gonna make copies of this thing?" Shawn asked after we went over the outline of the zine once again.

"My mom works at the copy center at the university," I reminded him. "I'll ask her if she'll make copies for us."

"But how are you gonna type up your parts? You don't have a laptop, do you?"

"I was just going to write it out by hand."

"No offense, Sydney." He pushed his glasses up his nose. "But I've seen your handwritin' and it's pretty, er, horrific."

"Hey!" I said in mock outrage. It was true. My handwriting wasn't the greatest. Just then I saw Ms. Yancey walking by, pushing a cart of books toward the graphic novel section. "Hold on. I've got an idea."

The bell was about to ring, so I grabbed my backpack and told Shawn I'd talk to him later. I went looking for Ms. Yancey. I found her kneeling down, shoving a graphic novel into an already crammed shelf. "What can I do for you, Sydney?"

"Shawn and I are thinking about putting together a zine, and I was wondering if I could use one of the library computers to type up my articles for it."

She cocked an eyebrow when she looked up. "Something tells me that this isn't part of a school assignment, is it?"

"Er, no, not exactly."

"Hmmm, and do I dare ask what it might be for?" She reached for another book to shelve.

"We're putting together a zine to raise awareness about the asphalt plant."

Ms. Yancey stopped what she was doing and looked at me closely for a second. "What exactly are you planning to include in this zine?"

I told her what Shawn and I had discussed.

"Will you be saying anything about the Winter family?"

"Well, I was going to write up a summary of what happened at the zoning committee meeting. The Winter brothers were both there."

She stood up and crossed her arms against her chest. Her expression was inscrutable. After a second, she shook her head. "Sydney, I can't have you using the school computers to write anything about the Winter family."

I started to argue, but she shook her head again.

"Nope. Don't argue with me, Sydney. That's just not going to happen. But I'll strike a deal with you. If you promise me you won't write anything about the Winters, then you can use the library computers. But when you do, just come see me so that I can log you on to my account. Okay?"

"Okay, thanks. But why do you always want me to use your account? Wouldn't it be easier for me to use my own?"

It often seemed like Ms. Yancey was having internal debates about what she felt she could say to me, and she was doing it again now. After a few moments she said, "Let's just say, it'd be better to have things on my account than on yours."

As I left the library, I chuckled to myself about how paranoid Ms. Yancey sounded.

But maybe she wasn't being paranoid at all.

Maybe she knew something I didn't.

When I got home that afternoon, I couldn't decide whether to work on my zine articles or my English assignment. But before I could do either, Granny set a big mug of hot chocolate down in front of me. As well as a letter from Kris. Okay, it wasn't even a letter. It was a postcard.

Hey, Syd! How are things? Greetings from Niagara Falls! Stef, Stu, their parents, and I went to Toronto for the weekend. We stopped off here to do the tourist thing. It is so cold!! Stu says 'hi.' xo Kris

After weeks of not hearing from her, she sends me a postcard? She went on vacation to Niagara Falls and all I got was a lousy postcard?!

Whatever. In the past, that would have bothered me. I tossed the postcard aside and started writing about the asphalt plant.

Ms. Yancey was sitting behind her desk when I walked into the library the next day. She nodded to me. "Sydney, I've logged on to that first computer, in case you want to use it for anything."

"Okay, thanks. Let me just set down my stuff and I'll be back in a minute."

But when I made my way back to the usual table, I was surprised to see Rita sitting with Shawn. I hadn't seen her for days.

"Oh, er, hi," I said, setting down my backpack.

"Hi." She looked rough. Like she hadn't slept in weeks.

Shawn was looking more nervous and uncomfortable than usual, which was saying something.

"Rita was just tellin' me about why she hasn't been in school the past few days."

"You haven't been here?" I said, surprised.

"Thanks for noticing."

"Well, sorry," I said, slightly wounded. "I just thought you were avoiding me because you were mad at me. Have you been sick? You look terrible."

"Thanks a lot, jerk," she snapped. "No, I wasn't sick."

You may be surprised to hear that sometimes I speak before thinking. I wanted to make things better with Rita, and here I was making things worse.

"Sorry. I'm sorry." And I meant it. "Look, I'll just stop talking now, okay?"

Shawn shot me a look that said I should have shut up ages ago.

Rita looked down at her hands clenched together on the table. I could see her bottom lip shaking. She was on the verge of tears. I hadn't realized how upset she was.

Shawn reached over and put his right hand on top of her clutched hands. I could see that Rita drew strength from that and for the first time I realized what a deep friendship they had. Before I crashed into their lives, they had only each other, hunkered back here in the corner of the library. Looking at them now, I felt outside of their close bond, but also within their circle of friendship. It was weird. They were best buddies; I was just second string. But I was the only one on the second string, and there was no other string after that. Any jealousy I felt about not being party to their closeness faded away with appreciation for the friendship that I did have with both of them.

"My father has cancer."

I felt a queasy, icy feeling take over my stomach.

"Oh my God, I'm so sorry." Instinctively, I reached out and put my hand on top of theirs.

Kris's mom had been diagnosed with cancer three years ago. She had done the full treatment, and as far as I knew, her cancer was still in remission. But I remembered how hard the diagnosis and the treatment had been on Kris's family. For a long stretch of time Kris didn't know if her mom was going to die or not. It was horrible.

I started to say something about Kris's experience, but fortunately this time I thought before speaking. Rita didn't want to hear about Kris. This was her experience. Her trauma. I needed to be there for her.

The three of us sat at our little table, our hands clasped together, while Rita told us the details. Her father had gone to the medical clinic a few weeks ago for a bad cough that wasn't going away. At first they thought it might just be bronchitis, but the test results raised all sorts of alarms. It looked like cancer, but they wanted to be sure. They sent him to the university hospital, and the scans showed that he had tumors throughout his lungs. He was still there, beginning some aggressive treatment. Rita and her mom had been staying with her dad in the hospital for the past several days.

"Oh, Rita, I'm so sorry." I squeezed her hands.

"Thanks."

"And listen, I'm really sorry I was such a jerk-butt the other day. It's just that I was frustrated and missing home. I'm sorry."

"Well, you *were* a jerk-butt," she said. "You know, I'm not your friend Kris, okay? I never will be."

"I know, I know. I was out of line. I'm sorry about that," I said, and I meant it so much.

She looked at me for a second before responding, "That's okay." Her voice sounded weak and exhausted.

"You know, Papa never smoked a day in his life. Mama is convinced that he got the cancer from either working in the fields with all the pesticides or working on the roads." She looked up at me. I knew what she was thinking. The research I had shared with them about asphalt indicated that prolonged exposure can cause cancer. Now her dad was a possible addition to those statistics.

"It's probably a combination of both, but it's impossible to prove any connection." She wiped her eyes with the back of her hand and took a deep breath. "Regardless, I'd like to help you with your campaign against the asphalt plant, if I can."

"Are you sure? You've got a lot going on at home, and..." I glanced tentatively at Shawn to make sure I wasn't saying anything inappropriate. "I know the stakes are different for us."

Rita shook her head, "It's the least I can do. But to be honest, I'm not sure what we can do."

Shawn smiled. "We're gonna fight them through the power of," dropping his voice in a low growl, "punk rock."

We explained to Rita the plan to make a zine and posters about the asphalt plant and put them around town. I told them that Ms. Yancey was letting me use her account on the library computers. When I mentioned her paranoia, Shawn nodded and said she probably had her reasons. He then added, turning to Rita, "But don't worry, my main job is to proofread all of Sydney's writing!"

Rita laughed. "Well, thank goodness for that. I've heard horror stories about how bad it is."

"Hey!" I replied in mock outrage, leaning toward Shawn as if I was gonna punch him. He emitted a high-pitched squeak and covered his head with his arms. His wussiness was so predictable, it almost wasn't fun to torture him like that. Almost.

"I know what I can do," Rita said. Shawn and I both looked over at her. "I can translate everything into Spanish, so we have Spanish language versions of the zine and the posters."

"Oh, Rita! That's a brilliant idea."

Things were starting to shape up nicely.

Over the next week, the three of us worked on the zine. I wrote out my essays and did a four-page spread of newspaper headlines about some of the numerous lawsuits against HD Dunkirk Industries. Shawn printed out maps to show

the site of the proposed asphalt plant for people who might
not know. We didn't mention the Winter family at all. We
figured that people would probably know who owned the
land. Shawn provided an amazingly well-written and concise
history of the area, all the way back to the time of the Native
American inhabitants. He also went to the Historical Society
and got some old photos that we could use.

My essays took the longest to finish because I would
give Shawn what I wrote and he'd come back with a heavily
edited version. When he gave it back to me, he went over
each sentence to explain what he changed and why. At first I
got annoyed because it felt like he was rubbing my mistakes
into my face. After the first few sentences, I felt my cheeks
burning from the embarrassment. But Shawn was patient
and kind. I realized that he was trying to help me learn from
my mistakes. I begrudgingly accepted that since he was a
genius, I should probably listen to what he was saying. It was
worth it. I think I learned more from him than any English
teacher.

We ended up printing everything out on the library computers. Then we shrank them down on the copier and pasted
them on blank pages so we could see what it would look like.
Because it takes a little bit of math to know how the pages
line up, we had to redo things a few times. But in the end, we
had a nice looking sixteen-page zine laid out on four pieces
of paper (each piece having four zine pages, two on the front
and two on the back). We had to do the whole thing again
with Rita's Spanish translation of the essays. I assumed she
did a great job, since I couldn't understand much of what she
had written. But I trusted her completely.

We also made a poster to hang up around town. It was
like a mini version of the zine. Just a short summary of the
dangers of the asphalt plant and a few headlines about HD
Dunkirk Industries.

The cover of the zine just had the words "NO ASPHALT

PLANT IN BEAVER DAM" in big letters. We put that at the top of the poster as well.

We were in the library putting the finishing touches on the poster when Ms. Yancey walked by. She had checked up on us regularly as we were working on the zine. She'd read what we had written, nod, then continue on without saying anything. She knew what were doing but was neither stopping us nor helping us.

"Implausible deniability" was what Shawn called it.

Rita laughed, "I think you mean 'plausible deniability.'"

"No. What she's doing is implausible. Nobody would believe she wasn't somehow involved. She's not doing anything, so she can't be held directly responsible. But it is clear she knows what we're doin' and is being supportive. She's walking a fine line."

As we were finishing the poster, Ms. Yancey finally broke her silence. "So, what are people supposed to do?"

"Um, get upset about it. Get angry," I said.

"Of course, I get that. But what do they do with that anger? What are you asking them to do exactly?"

I hadn't thought about that. I wanted to raise people's awareness, which was the first challenge I had mentioned to Shawn. But now Ms. Yancey was pointing out the second challenge: overcoming that feeling of powerlessness.

"Um, I'm not really sure," I admitted.

Shawn, Rita, and I looked at each other. I could feel our confidence dropping rapidly.

Ms. Yancey cleared her throat. "Well, if I could make a suggestion?"

I looked at her hopefully. "Please do."

"You can create a petition for people to sign. It could oppose the asphalt plant and call for a referendum on the issue."

Shawn looked at her. "A referendum?"

"Yes. That's when people get to vote on whether

something should be a law. It just so happens that in Beaver Dam, if ten percent of the voters call for a referendum on any matter, the county commission has to hold one. Since there are roughly five thousand registered voters living in the county, you'd need to get at least 500 residents to sign the petition. If the majority vote in favor of the referendum, it becomes law."

We all looked at Ms. Yancey, stunned.

"Just sayin'," she added, with a sly smile.

"That's a brilliant idea!" I gasped.

So we set out writing the petition. Shawn suggested we keep it brief, so people wouldn't be scared off by having to read too much. In the end, this is what we came up with:

We, the undersigned, oppose the building of an asphalt plant on Laurel Ridge Road and call upon the Beaver Dam County Commission to hold a referendum banning the construction of all asphalt plants within the county.

Underneath, we had spaces where people could add their signatures, along with their names and addresses. Ms. Yancey pointed out that the people had to be residents of the county for their signature to count.

When we were finished, I took the zine, the poster, and the petition home and asked Mom if she'd be willing to make copies at the university's printing center. At first she seemed unsure. But before she could say no, Granny interrupted. She'd already read over everything that afternoon when I brought the zine home. She'd hugged me and told me how proud she was of me.

"You'll be happy to, won't you, Aubrey? And if it is a matter of cost, I'll be happy to pay for it."

Mom looked at Granny for a second, then nodded and turned to me. "Of course, sweetie. I'll be happy to. I can make the copies at work tomorrow and bring them home in the evening."

Granny piped up again. "And on Saturday, Harold can

drive Sydney 'round town to distribute 'em. Won't you, Harold?"

Grandpop had been reading the paper by the woodstove and looked up at the sound of his name. Granny repeated what she had said. It was clear that she was making a statement more than asking a question. Grandpop took the hint.

"Sure. I've got some errands to run, both here and in Franklin. Sydney and I can spend the day drivin' 'round."

Granny looked over at me and winked. I guess my ban from Franklin had been lifted.

Saturday morning, Grandpop and I drove around Beaver Dam, putting up posters and setting out zines for people to take. When I found a community bulletin board, I would thumbtack the poster up, with a copy of the petition attached below. But when we went into stores, we'd ask the owner for permission to hang up the poster and petition.

Well, Grandpop asked. Often he knew the owner personally. But after glancing over the poster, almost all of them looked uncomfortable and declined. Grandpop told them he understood and left without pushing the point.

We were getting so many rejections that I was starting to get depressed.

The little bell attached to the door of the old hardware store chimed when we walked in. It had a smell I think only old hardware stores have: a comforting blend of wood, metal, oil, and age. The owner was standing alone behind the front counter, flipping through what looked like a paint catalog. Grandpop greeted him—turns out his name was Everett—and explained why we were there. Everett squinted at the poster and the petition closely, his lips moving as he read the whole thing. When he finished, he looked from Grandpop to me and then back again.

"That's Winter's property, ain't it?"

"I s'pose it is," Grandpop said, without displaying any emotion.

"Ain't many people gonna put their name on a piece of paper that goes against them Winter boys."

I fidgeted next to Grandpop. I had suspected that this had been the issue with the folks who refused to accept the poster and petition.

"Can't say what people might do, or why," Grandpop said.

"Nope. I guess that's true enough," agreed Everett, looking back at the poster and petition. "But I s'pose given the choice, most folks'll keep their heads down and their butts covered." He set the petition down on the counter, took out a pen from his shirt pocket, and signed the top line, adding his name and address. "I agree with the cause, missy." He looked over at me. "But stickin' it to them little sons-of-a-turd makes it even sweeter."

As we left, Everett was putting the poster and petition in a prominent place on his checkout counter. Getting into the pickup truck, Grandpop remarked that we could use more Everetts in this world.

I had to agree.

Mom had made 250 copies of the English language version of the zine and fifty of the Spanish version. Rita had taken all of the Spanish language ones to distribute and Shawn had taken fifty of the ones in English. I had taken the rest and left a little stack in every place I could in Beaver Dam.

I had about twenty-five copies of the zine left, as well as a few posters, when we drove to Franklin. I hadn't planned on leaving any there, since it wasn't in the same county as Beaver Dam. But then Grandpop suggested we pay a visit to Cherryhill Books and Records.

Ben was behind the counter when we walked in and seemed happy to see us.

"Hey there, Sydney! Howdy, Mr. Avery. It's been a while."

I explained to him that I'd been grounded because of a bad grade.

For some reason he found that funny.

I also told him how much I liked the Ward Cleavers album that he'd given me, especially "Mountain Laurel."

"Yeah, that's a great song. That's one of the songs that Betty wrote. I knew it was a keeper the first time she played it for me."

"I even told Dani of Lite Brite about y'all and she loves that song too."

"You told Dani DeLite about us? No way! That's so cool."

He noticed the zines and posters in my hand and asked what they were. I told him the story of how Rita, Shawn, and I had put them together to raise people's awareness of the proposed asphalt plant by our school. I asked if I could put up a poster and maybe leave a few zines. He agreed and started flipping through the zine as I flipped through the crate of new releases.

"This is really good, Sydney. How many copies of these do you have left?"

"About twenty-five, I think."

"I'll take 'em all. I think the clientele here would be totally into this. And give me a few extra posters. I can put 'em around Franklin in places that I think'll make a difference."

"But only local residents can sign the petition," I pointed out.

"I don't think that matters. It's about getting the word out. And you'd be surprised how many people from Beaver Dam come over to Franklin."

I gave him all the rest of my zines and posters. He put the zines right by the cash register, along with a poster and the petition taped to the counter. He put another poster by the front door.

Grandpop had been looking through the bluegrass and country albums in the back. When he walked up to the front, he said, "That's like flippin' through my own record collection. Do people really buy that old stuff?"

"You'd be surprised, Mr. Avery."

"Call me Harold. Please."

"Well, Harold, they aren't my best sellers. But they are consistent sellers, if you know what I mean. I may have a Doc Watson or Louvin Brothers album for a couple of months. But then that one person is gonna walk in the door and flip their lid when they see it. They know what it's worth and aren't bothered about paying it."

"Well, heck, I should bring in my collection for you to sell."

"I'd be happy to buy them off you, Harold, if you're serious 'bout gettin' rid of 'em. But I think you'd be making a better investment by givin' 'em to Sydney."

Grandpop laughed. "Yep, get her to stop listenin' to that noise of hers and appreciate some good music."

Ben smiled. "All good music sounds like noise to those who don't know better."

Grandpop smiled back at him. "I suppose that's so."

He reached over and messed up my hair.

I had distributed all the posters and zines.

Things were starting to look up.

And then Monday happened.

12

Monday morning brought the bitter cold. A mix of snow and fog made the bus ride to school slow and treacherous. Looking out the window, I saw thick fluffy flakes coming down in front of a billowy backdrop of snow. Occasionally the fog would lift and expose a rolling hillside under a thick white blanket. It was gorgeous, but it also meant we got to school later than usual.

I had to rush to my locker before going to Mrs. Critcher's social studies class. I saw Bethany and the clueless clique lingering in the hallway but didn't think anything about it at first. But when I opened my locker, a huge shower of confetti fell out, scattering all over the floor. A cackle of laughter erupted behind me, leaving no doubt as to who had done it.

"Oh, look, there's a blizzard in Vicious Sydney's locker. Is it snow, or has her dandruff gotten out of control?" Further cackling.

The confetti covered everything inside my locker. All over my books and folders, spilling out onto the floor and covering my shoes as well.

Bethany stepped behind me and, in a much lower and more menacing voice, said, "Take this as a warning." And she and her mimeographed minions walked off toward Mrs. Critcher's class laughing.

I dragged over a garbage can and started scooping up the confetti. After a few handfuls, I realized that the confetti was actually the posters and petitions that I had put up around town that weekend. They had been shredded into tiny bits and stuffed into my locker.

"How did they even get into your locker?" Rita said, with a mix of concern and confusion.

"I have no idea. But I'm sure they didn't just slip each piece through a crack at the top. They definitely opened up the locker, spread it all around, and then set it up a box that was rigged to spill out when I opened the locker door. It was pretty ingenious, actually. I may have underestimated Bethany's intelligence."

Shawn looked up. "We don't know it was Bethany."

Rita and I both stared at him incredulously. "Really?" we asked in unison.

"Okay, fine, we can make a pretty safe bet that it was Bethany."

"You said she called it a 'warning'?" Rita asked.

"Yeah. I guess she went around town pulling the posters and petitions down. Probably with her dad."

"That's a lot of work. And a good sign," added Rita.

"How is destroying all of our posters a good sign?"

"Well, if she and her dad saw them and didn't feel threatened, they would have just left them up. But the fact that they went to all that trouble shows that they are taking this as a serious challenge," Rita said.

"Hmm, that makes sense," Shawn said, adjusting his glasses. "So what do we do now?"

Before I could answer, Rita responded, "Keep doing what we're doing. If they are tearing the posters down, we'll just put more up. We've got to show them that we're not scared and we're not to be messed with."

I had underestimated Rita's tenacity. I smiled at her. "Remind me never to get on your bad side."

Rita smiled back. It felt great to be back on good terms with her. A wave of warmth passed over me. I had forgotten what it was like to have friends.

"But what about the petitions? What do we do about those?" Shawn asked.

Rita thought for a second. "We could create an online petition. We could list the website on the posters directing people where to go to sign it. If it's online, it would be protected. People couldn't rip it up."

It was a brilliant idea, but we had no idea how to go about putting it into action. How does one create an online petition? So I went looking for Ms. Yancey, who was eating a pack of crackers at her desk. When I explained what had happened to our original petitions, she was visibly disturbed. "Someone went around town and tore them all down?"

"Yes, and then that 'someone' shredded them all, got access to my locker, and stuffed them inside."

Ms. Yancey looked at me closely. "Do you know for sure who that 'someone' was?"

"Well, a super annoying 'someone' and her pathetic posse were standing behind me when I opened my locker and that 'someone' told me that it was a warning."

"I see. And now you want to create an online petition, instead of paper ones?"

"Yeah, but we're not sure how we go about doing that. Can you help us?"

"Well, it's easy to create an online petition. There are websites that we can use. But it probably wouldn't be wise to have my name attached to this." I knew better than to ask why not, but she seemed to need to offer an explanation. "I've only been here at the school for a few months. I'm still in my probation period."

We all liked Ms. Yancey and didn't want her to get in trouble. If Bethany had gotten into my locker, someone probably helped her. For my money, it was probably Mr. Snead. Ms. Yancey might have had good reason to have been paranoid all along.

She looked thoughtful for a minute. "You should see if Steve Snead will do it."

I'm pretty sure my eyeballs briefly popped out of my head. If I had been drinking anything at that moment, it would have sprayed out of my nose and all over Ms. Yancey.

"Snead? *The* Mr. Snead?"

Ms. Yancey arched an eyebrow at me. "Is there something wrong, Sydney?"

"Uh, no, not really. I'm just not sure why we should ask Mr. Snead, that's all."

"Well, Mr. Snead is active with environmental issues throughout the region. He is the head of the local Green Party. He'd be the person most people would expect to create a petition like this."

"Well, it's just that, er, I don't think he likes me very much. So I'm not sure he'd be willing to do it."

Ms. Yancey smiled. "Well, why don't you ask him, and find out?"

"I think that might be a really bad idea."

"What if I put in a good word for you?"

I begrudgingly agreed. I didn't have Mr. Snead's English class until the next day, so I told Ms. Yancey that I'd ask him them. She said she'd try to butter him up beforehand.

I didn't say it, but I doubted that there was enough butter in the universe for mean Mr. Snead.

For my English project, I had decided to write an essay on *King Lear*, arguing that Lear felt his masculinity threatened because he was dependent on his daughters to take care of him. I had bounced a few ideas off Rita at school and was feeling pretty good about how my paper was shaping up. Rita had shared a few stories about how her sick dad was dealing with being so dependent on her and her mom, so she thought I was making insightful arguments. I was in my room, thinking about how to structure the conclusion of my essay when I heard Granny calling from downstairs, telling me I had a phone call.

I didn't know who it could be. Joey only called on Sundays to check in. If it was Mom, Granny would have said so. Shawn and Rita never called. I don't think they even had my phone number. I immediately jumped to the conclusion that it must be something to do with Bethany. Maybe she was calling to threaten me again.

But it turned out to be Ben from Cherryhill Books and Records.

"Hey! How did you get my number?"

"I remembered your grandfather's name was Harold Avery, so I looked it up. Turns out that there's only one Harold Avery in Beaver Dam."

"So what's up?" I asked, slightly confused as to why Ben was calling me.

"You know those zines you left with me on Saturday?"

"Uh, yeah." Now I was confused *and* worried. Had something bad happened? Had I gotten Ben in trouble with the petition?

"I need more copies."

"Wait, what?"

"I ran out a few hours after you left. And all day today I've had people comin' in and askin' if I have any more copies left."

"Seriously?" I couldn't believe it.

"Yeah, seriously. I'll take as many as you can get me. And I'm happy to cover the cost. Most of the people comin' in have never been in before, so it's been great for business. Seriously, can you get me a hundred copies? Better make it two hundred."

I agreed to bring more copies to him in the next few days. I told him about moving the petition online and how we were going to list the website in the zine. We'd just paste a little line on the back cover. After we got an online petition established, that was.

"That's great, because the petition you left is already full. I created a second page, but that's almost full now too."

"Are they all from residents of Beaver Dam?" I asked in disbelief.

"Yeah, pretty sure they are. All the addresses listed are in your county."

Holy crudola.

Since Mr. Snead hated me, I asked Shawn to go with me after class. Even though he was a big wuss, Shawn agreed to do most of the talking since Snead liked him more.

"Mr. Snead, do you have a minute?" Shawn said nervously as we approached him at his desk.

"Of course, Mr. Tucker. What can I do for you?" Then, as Mr. Snead looked up and saw me standing beside Shawn, he added "Ah yes, Ms. Yancey said you might be stopping by."

I had been quiet for a full fifteen seconds. I figured that had been long enough. "Did she explain why we wanted to talk to you?"

"She did." He sounded both exhausted and annoyed. "You want me to create an online petition for your campaign against the proposed asphalt plant, correct?"

Shawn shot me a warning look to remind me that I should let him do the talking.

"Yes, sir."

I looked at Shawn, waiting for him to say more, but that seemed to be the extent of his sales pitch. So I started in. "This is important, Mr. Snead. The asphalt plant would be highly dangerous, environmentally speaking, for Beaver Dam and especially the school."

"Yes, yes." He reached into his leather briefcase and took out a copy of our zine. "I've read all about it."

He flipped through the zine and then looked up at us. "I am assuming you wrote this together. If I may say so, it is a step above your usual standards, Miss Talcott." Looking from me to Shawn, he added, "And quite below yours, Mr. Tucker."

I didn't know who should be more offended, Shawn or me.

"Well, will you do it?" I asked, a little snottily, if truth be told.

"I've already done it. Here is the website for the petition." He handed over a piece of paper with a URL written down. "I also took the liberty of letting some people know about it. I believe there are a few dozen signatures on the petition already."

"Um, thanks!" I said, slightly stunned.

"Yes. And if you have some extra copies of your little publication, I wouldn't mind several dozen more."

"Uh, of course," Shawn said. "Thank you, Mr. Snead. We appreciate it."

He looked at me, slightly dismissively I thought, and replied, "Yes. I'm sure you do."

Shawn took me by the arm and dragged me out of the classroom.

We high-fived in the hallway.

Ben had been adamant about giving me money for the new copies of the zine. Mom was willing to cover the cost of printing another hundred copies, as well as a new batch of posters, which also listed the petition's website. She brought them home later in the week. Shawn dropped twenty-five off with Mr. Snead. Ms. Yancey also took another twenty-five.

Saturday morning, Grandpop and I drove back around Beaver Dam, putting up new posters and leaving a few zines around. The petition at Everett's was full, as was a second sheet of paper that he had taped atop the original. A third sheet already had five signatures.

"Gimme some more of them little booklets, if you got any," he said when we gave him an updated poster. "Plenty people comin' in askin' for 'em."

So we left him a few dozen, before heading to Franklin with the two hundred copies for Ben.

"Howdy, Sydney. Howdy, Harold," Ben called out from

behind the counter as we walked in. Two college students were waiting by the register. The girl had a Grateful Dead album, while the guy standing behind her had what looked like a small stack of Pink Floyd albums. Not my cup of tea, but I knew from Ben that these were the types of purchases that kept Cherryhill in business, at least the record-shop half.

Grandpop wandered off to the bookstore side while I waited for Ben to ring up his customers. "Were you able to bring me more copies of your zine?" he asked, after the Pink Floyd dude left.

"Sure did." I pointed to the box I'd set down by the door. "Because we moved the petition online, I've got new posters with the URL on it."

"That's a great idea to put it online." Ben came out behind the counter to pick up the box of zines.

"Well, we didn't have much of a choice." I told him the story of the shredded petitions in my locker from earlier in the week. He responded with a mixture of outrage and laughter. But mostly laughter.

"Man, whoever did that has some serious anger issues. I guess you struck a raw nerve. Good going!"

"Yeah, I'm 100 percent certain it was Bradley Winter's daughter, Bethany, who did it. But she probably had help from someone at the school. They had to unlock my locker in order to put that stuff in there."

"Huh. I hadn't thought about that. I know Bradley Winter is pretty influential in Beaver Dam. I don't think he owns anything over here in Franklin."

"Yet."

"Yeah, I guess that's right. I s'pose it is only a matter of time."

Grandpop wandered back into the record store side of the building, so I said I should probably be going.

"Hold on, let me pay you for this new batch of zines." He fished out some cash from the register.

"Thanks, we appreciate the help. And just call me if you ever need any more copies."

"I will. Also, I've got one more thing for you." He turned around to the shelf behind him and shuffled through some papers and folders. "Ah, here it is."

He turned around with a big manila envelope and opened it up.

"You know my bandmate Betty? She was so inspired by your zine, she made you this."

In his hand was a drawing of a little girl, with a teddy bear in one hand and the other holding onto the strap of a book bag slung over her shoulder. She had two pigtails that stuck out from either side of her head. But you couldn't see her face, because she had a big gas mask on. Underneath the drawing, in handwritten block letters, it said NO ASPHALT PLANT IN BEAVER DAM.

"Ohmygod, that is amazing!"

"Yeah, Betty's a great artist. This is the original. But she made a copy and wanted me to ask you if she could make some T-shirts with that image on it."

Grandpop had walked up next to me and was also admiring the drawing. "How's she gonna be able to do that?"

"She just makes a silk screen out of it," Ben replied. But seeing that Grandpop didn't understand, he explained how the silk-screen process worked. "In her case, she redraws the image on a screen that has a wooden frame. Then she places the screen on a blank T-shirt and runs ink 'cross the screen. The ink goes through where she drew, so the image gets transferred onto the shirt. Then she uses a hair dryer to dry the ink. She does all the band's merchandise, but she also makes shirts and clothes as a hobby. That's some of her stuff up there."

He pointed to a number of shirts hanging on the wall. A few had the Cherryhill logo, but most had other cool designs, including one with a cat sitting in a tree and another with the outline of a mountain range.

"Betty said she'd love to make some shirts of the gas mask girl and we could sell 'em here at the store. All the money would go to you for the campaign against the asphalt plant. Plus, she'll give you a bunch to hand out to your friends and family."

"That'd be awesome! I'd love that. But we don't have a bank account or money for this campaign."

"Well, you might wanna start one. It'd be good to build up a little war chest for the cause. You can use the funds to print more zines and posters, or whatever else. I'll let Betty know that you're cool with her makin' shirts. Stop by in a few days and I'm sure I'll have some in by then. Betty is pretty fast, plus she's fired up about this issue."

As we said our goodbyes, Ben added, "I'll see if I can get you and Betty together sometime soon. Y'all would dig each other. She's like an older version of you, but with a super-thick mountain accent."

As Grandpop pushed the door open, he mused, "That sounds like a dangerous combination."

On Monday, there wasn't any confetti in my locker. But it took almost an hour to find that out, because someone had glued the door shut. The janitor had to pry it open with a crowbar. When he was finished, the door was so bent the locker no longer closed.

Mrs. Fletcher seemed convinced that it was my fault when she called me down to her office later that morning to assign me a new locker. "I don't know what you did to that poor locker, Miss Talcott, but I expect you to treat school property with a bit more respect." She looked at me over the reading glasses perched on the end of her nose.

"What? You think I did this to my own locker?"

"Well, what else do you suggest?"

"Only an idiot would think I'd glue my own locker shut. Why would I do that?"

"I certainly wouldn't know, Miss Talcott. Which is why I am asking you. Even though I may be an *idiot* for doing so."

"Why don't you ask Bethany? I'm sure she was behind this, just like when she put the confetti in my locker last week."

"Unless you have proof for such an outrageous accusation, I suggest you refrain from defaming Bethany Winter or any other Beaver Dam students. The fact of the matter is, Miss Talcott," she said, taking her glasses off and giving me the sternest look she could, "nothing of this sort has ever happened at this school. That is, until *you* got here."

"What? Do you think that I filled my own locker up with confetti? That I glued my own locker closed? That is insane."

"Miss Talcott, in the last minute you have called me insane and an idiot. I am willing to excuse such outbursts for the time being. But rest assured that we've got our eyes on you."

I wondered whom she meant by the "we," but I wasn't going to press my luck. I didn't think she was an idiot or insane, but I was beginning to suspect that she might be more than a little dangerous. Plus, I wanted to get out of there before I blew my cool. The last thing I needed right now was for my internal Joan Jett to get me into more trouble. Granny would definitely have grounded me for life.

On Wednesday, Rita wasn't at lunch. Shawn said that he hadn't seen her all day. We worried that her father's situation had deteriorated. The next day, we found out that her dad was doing okay. But she'd missed school because of something equally serious. "Immigration has been raiding apartment buildings and trailer parks across Beaver Dam," Rita said when she joined us in the library on Thursday.

"Holy crudola."

"Yeah. They've detained at least six families so far, including one from my building."

Shawn looked worried. "That's awful. What prompted this, do you think?"

"You can guess what prompted it. Supposedly they were asking people about the Spanish version of our zine."

"No way!" I exclaimed.

"That's what I hear. I gave out all of the copies we had, so it's been circulating in the community. I understand the immigration agents were asking people where it came from. They even took it from my neighbor's apartment when they questioned her and her family."

"What did they say to you?"

"Who, immigration? They didn't talk to me. They raided our building on Tuesday. I was in school during the day, and then went to see dad in the hospital. When we got back home, we heard the news. My mom took off work yesterday, and she and I drove around the county checking on people. Momma's active in our church, so people trust her."

I didn't know what to say. It seemed shocking that the immigration authorities would be targeting people because of our zine. But Shawn didn't seem that surprised.

"I'm sure immigration doesn't care 'bout the zine. I imagine they're probably doing a favor for the Winter family in return for whatever favor they are doing for them. It's just how things work 'round here. A powerful family like the Winters can get people to do things for them."

"Like round up poor immigrants," Rita said.

"Or break into students' lockers," I said. "Not that they are the same thing at all. My point is that they can do things, both big and small, to make their power felt."

Rita nodded. "I know what you meant. And if this is about intimidating people, it's working. Driving around the county yesterday, we talked to a lot of scared folks."

Shawn looked at her with concern. "What about you? Are you scared?"

"I'd be stupid not to be. But I've never seen my momma so angry as I did yesterday. She's more angry than scared, and I think that's a good way to be."

Rita looked over at me. "In fact, she wants a bunch more of our asphalt zines, in Spanish and English. She wants people to know what this is about and what's at stake."

"Wow. Your mom's kind of a...a..."

I was searching for the right expression.

"A *tía dura.*"

"*Sí.*" Rita smiled at me. "Yes, she is."

Granny and Grandpop were sitting at the kitchen table when I got home that afternoon. They had two cups of tea in front of them, and at first I didn't notice the letter on the table.

"Is there any more tea?" I asked as I came in and took my snowy boots off.

"There's some in the pot," said Granny.

When I sat down with them at the table with my mug,

Grandpop looked over at Granny. "Do you wanna tell her or shall I?"

Granny sighed. "Well, we hadn't agreed to tell her, had we?"

"Tell me what? What's going on?" Seeing the letter on the table, my stomach flipped. It looked official and I imagined it was from the school. Probably from Mrs. Fletcher, suspending me for vandalizing my own locker.

Granny shot Grandpop a look. "Well, I guess we have to tell her now, don't we?" Grandpop just shrugged slightly. Granny turned toward me. "It is nothing for you to worry about, sweetheart, but we received this letter today." She held it up with disgust, as if she'd wiped up cat poop with it. "The zoning commission is lettin' us know that they're considerin' puttin' a road through our property."

"What? That's crazy. They can't do that!"

"Unfortunately, they can," Grandpop said. "It's called 'eminent domain.' It means the government can take any land they feel is necessary for development, as long as they compensate the owners. It happens all the time."

Granny looked like she could spit nails. "It's just them Winter boys tryin' to scare us off."

I picked up the letter and looked it over. I was too upset to take it all in and most of it was over my head anyway. Specific coordinates were listed, but it didn't make any sense to me. "I don't understand what this means. Where exactly is this road supposed to go?"

Grandpop seemed calmer than Granny, who clearly wanted to punch something or somebody. He said, "They wanna build a short road about half a mile long, whose only purpose seems to be that it'll go directly behind our house and through the back gardens."

"Those Winter boys aren't gonna get away with this," Granny fumed. "We'll fight this."

"Of course we will. But that's also what they're hoping

we'll do. We'll have to sue the county and that means expensive legal fees. They're hopin' to wear us down and bleed us dry."

"Why are they doing this?" But I didn't need to ask. We'd declared war on the asphalt plant, and now the Winters were declaring war on us. The confetti in my locker had been a warning. But now the stakes had increased dramatically. For Rita, her family and her friends. And now for Granny and Grandpop as well.

My stomach hurt.

Dinner was a quiet affair. As usual, Mom wasn't there. Grandpop was even more silent than usual. He'd told me that everything would be fine, but I could tell he was worried. Granny spent most of the dinner cursing the Winters under her breath. I learned a few new expressions and was impressed by her creativity in coming up with new swear words. "Bottom-feeding pig pee-sniffers" might have been my favorite.

It wasn't until I was going upstairs to finish my homework that Granny remembered there had been a letter for me. I recognized Dani's handwriting on the envelope and took it upstairs with me.

Hey, Sydney!! I hope you are doing well. We've been buried under snow up here in Chicago for weeks now, but I think we're finally turning the corner and spring will be here soon. It better be!! I don't mind the winter weather at all, except when it overstays its welcome. How are things with you? You never said what grade you got on that paper about The Unbearable Lightness of Being a Girl. I'm sure you got a good grade. How are the rest of your classes going? I hope you are settling into the school OK. And how is the campaign against the asphalt plant going? Thanks so much for sending me a copy of that zine. Excellent job putting your DIY punk skills to good use! Seriously, it was really great. Lots of useful information. I learned so much about asphalt, Beaver Dam, and how horrible HD Dunkirk Industries is. If there is anything I can do to help, please let me know! And that brings me to ask YOU a favor. I've been putting together our May tour. We're gonna be on the road for over two weeks. Heading down the east coast, and then out to Texas, up to Colorado, and then back to Chicago. I had wanted to go all the way out to California and do the West Coast as well, but that would take another week and we can't be gone from work for that long. So the West Coast will have to wait until the fall. ANYWAY, we've got a small gap in the tour. We play Richmond on a Thursday and then Atlanta on Saturday. We were gonna play in Chapel Hill for that Friday, but that show has fallen through. I thought it might be cool if we drove up to Beaver Dam to visit you! Is there any chance you and your grandparents could put us all up? Yeah, I'm inviting ourselves to your place! I'm such a jerk, right? We can totally find a hotel to stay in if it is too much hassle to host us. But I've told the band all about you and we're all really interested in visiting Beaver Dam and meeting you. And if you have any suggestions of places to play nearby, maybe we can even get a show together. Let me know if this would work out. No worries if it doesn't. I'll totally understand. But I thought it'd be cool to stop by and see you.

xoxo DANI

At the bottom of the page, she'd done another self-portrait. This time she'd drawn herself playing her bass and singing into a microphone: "Hello Beaver Dam!"

And that's when the idea of the century hit me.

13

Y ou want to do *what* now?" Rita asked.
I had told Shawn and Rita about my idea as soon as
we sat down in the library.

"Hold a concert."

"But you said we weren't gonna form a band!" Shawn looked petrified at the idea.

I laughed. "Not us, bonehead. We're gonna get a couple of bands together to play a concert for the asphalt plant campaign. It'll help raise awareness about the issue, and we can use whatever extra money we raise to promote the petition campaign."

"But we don't know anything about putting on a concert," Rita said, taking tamales out of a Tupperware container.

"I've been to loads of DIY shows back in Rochester. It's not hard. You just have to find a space and line up a handful of bands. We'll need a PA system, but I'm sure one of the bands will have one we can use. Other than that, it's just a matter of getting the word out. We can sell tickets at the door."

"But what kind of space are you talking about?" Rita took a bite of her food. With her mouth full she continued, "There aren't any auditoriums or anything like that in Beaver Dam."

"Well, the school has an auditorium. We could see about using that space. If not, we can be creative. Most of the shows I went to in Rochester were basement shows, backyard parties or in church halls. They were all-age shows, which is great because that means anyone can come."

"Okay, setting aside the issue of where this would take place. What band would want to play in Beaver Dam? We don't even know any bands," Rita said.

"I do," I said. "And Lite Brite has offered to play."

"Really? You've already asked them?"

"Well, no. But they asked if I would put them up when they are passing through the area. And they asked for help finding them a show. I know they'd do it if I asked, especially because they are into our asphalt-plant campaign."

"No offense, Sydney," interrupted Shawn, halfway into his peanut butter and jelly sandwich. "I know you love 'em, but nobody else around here has probably even heard of Lite Brite. What makes you think people'll come out to see 'em play?"

"No offense taken, newbie. Let me hip you to some of the basic rules of putting on a DIY show. First, the headline band should be a bigger name band on tour. Not everyone might know them, so you then get two or three local bands to draw in a local crowd. So I'm thinking I could ask the Ward Cleavers to play as well."

Rita and Shawn looked at me blankly.

"They're a punk band from Franklin that combines traditional Appalachian music and instruments into their songs. They've got a big following in the area." I didn't actually know if that was true, but I was hoping it would be. "So they'd bring in loads of people from Franklin. Especially those who are fired up by the campaign against the asphalt plant."

Rita nodded slowly. "But what about a local band? What would encourage people in Beaver Dam to come to the show?"

I sat there for a minute thinking.

Then Shawn spoke up. "Does it have to be a punk band?"

"No, of course not. In fact, it'd be cool to mix up musical genres to get some diversity."

"Well, if that's the case, I think I may know a band who'd be willin' to play."

I looked at him in disbelief. "You know a band?"

"You're not the only cool one 'round here," he said in mock indignation. We all laughed. "It just so happens that I have two uncles and an aunt who have an Appalachian old-time music group. My aunt was really concerned about the asphalt plant when I was talkin' to her 'bout it. They haven't played out in a long time, but I could ask 'em if they'd be willin' to play. They'd be fun, especially if the Bored Cleaver play old-time music as well."

I laughed. "It's the Ward Cleavers, not the Bored Cleaver. You know, the father in *Leave it to Beaver*." Shawn looked at me blankly and then shrugged. "Whatever. Forget the reference," I said. "But we don't have many options. If your relatives are willing to play, I guess that would be cool. It would give us three bands. That's a decent lineup. We're on our way!"

Shawn said he'd ask his uncles and aunt that afternoon.

I was super stoked and could tell that the two of them were warming up to the idea. But Rita looked at me with her brow furrowed and asked, "We still don't have a space. Where are we going to do this?"

"Leave that to me. It'll be easy."

Mrs. Fletcher looked at me like I was crazy.

"Excuse me? What did you say?"

"I asked if it would be possible to use the school auditorium for a musical show," I said as sweetly as possible. I didn't mention anything about it being a punk show. I figured that proposal wouldn't get far.

She eyed me suspiciously. "What do you mean a show?"

"We're getting a few local musical acts together for a benefit concert, and we thought it would be great to hold it here at the school. It would be the school's chance to, you know, give back to the community."

"Uh-huh. And this would be a benefit for what exactly?"

"To raise awareness about the proposed asphalt plant."

Mrs. Fletcher looked like I had just slapped her across the face with a rotten fish. "Wha…wha…wha…"

"Well, since the asphalt plant will have a huge environmental impact on the health of the students, I thought it'd make sense for the school to show its concern."

"Are you crazy?" she said. "Absolutely not! We will not be party to any such event. No way."

"But Mrs. Fletcher…"

She was on her feet now, crossing around her desk toward me. She looked livid. I didn't know what she was about to do, but for a second I thought she might pick me up and throw me out the window. I jumped up and moved behind the chair in order to keep it between us. It was a first-floor window, but still.

She walked to the door and flung it open.

"You need to leave right now. There is no way this school will be involved in any such thing. I should suspend you for even suggesting it."

With the mention of a possible suspension, I was out the door and down the hall like a shot.

So that went worse than expected.

The next day at lunch, Shawn told us that his uncles and aunt, who went by the name the Tucker Trio, had agreed to play. I told them I'd written to Dani, asking if Lite Brite would be interested in playing at the benefit show. It would take her several days to write back, so we just had to wait. It was one of those times I hated not being able to use social media for the instant response.

Without going into the details, I told them Mrs. Fletcher declined my request to use the school auditorium.

"So where are we gonna hold the concert?" Shawn asked.

"Don't worry. I have a Plan B."

But I had no Plan B. At least, not yet.

I was hoping Ben might have a suggestion when I dropped

off another hundred copies of the zine at Cherryhill the following Saturday. He didn't. But he was excited about being asked to play.

"I am 99 percent certain that we can do that, but let me just double-check with the rest of the band. Thanks so much for askin' us. It'll be awesome to play with Lite Brite. But I'm sorry, I don't have a clue about where you could put on a show in Beaver Dam. If you want, we could organize something here in Franklin. But that'd pretty much defeat the purpose."

Grandpop was at the counter with me and before I could respond, he interjected. "Ben's right, Sydney. It needs to be in Beaver Dam, otherwise people'll feel it is a bunch of outsiders tellin' 'em what to do."

"Yeah. I guess y'all are right."

"I'll keep my thinkin' cap on, though," Ben added. "And I'll ask around."

I ended up buying a Neighborhood Brats album that Ben recommended, and Grandpop bought a Doc Watson album he said he'd always regretted not getting when he was younger. It was one Doc had done with his son Merle, who died tragically just as his own career started to take off. It turned out Grandpop had known Merle, so he and Ben swapped stories about the Watsons, who had lived just outside of Franklin.

Before we left, Ben remembered the box of T-shirts that Betty had dropped off earlier that morning.

Ben pulled out one of the T-shirts and it looked super awesome. The Gas-Mask Girl was in black ink, and NO ASPHALT PLANT IN BEAVER DAM was in a striking dark red.

Betty had told Ben I could take as many as I wanted. I was just going to get shirts for Rita, Shawn, and myself. But Grandpop then tried to pay for extra shirts for himself, Mom, and Granny.

"No way," Ben responded. "You can have those for free as well."

Grandpop and Ben argued for several minutes before they reached an agreement that Grandpop would buy four for the price of two. But when Ben took the money, he turned right around and handed it to me. "There you go, Sydney. Add it to the war chest. And if you come back next week, I guarantee you that I'll have sold a bunch of these."

When we left he was hanging up several of the shirts on the wall behind the counter. They looked so cool.

On the drive home, I asked Grandpop what he was going to do with the fourth shirt.

"Oh, that's a gift for a friend who'll no doubt wear it with pride. In fact, we can drop it off on our way home."

A little while later, we pulled up in front of Everett's hardware store. Everett was sitting on a stool behind the counter, flipping through another catalog. He looked up when the bell over the front door chimed.

"Afternoon, Harold. Missy." He nodded to me.

"Afternoon, Everett," Grandpop replied.

"Any chance you brought me some more of them li'l booklets? I believe I only got a couple left."

I told him that I had a dozen or so out in the truck and went out to get them. When I walked back in Everett was holding up the Gas Mask Girl T-shirt. "Yessir, I'll be wearin' this thing every chance I get. 'Specially when I'm shoppin' at the Harris Teeter."

I handed over the zines and Everett thanked me for them and the shirt, which he was continuing to admire with a little gleam in his eye. "How's the good fight goin', missy?"

I told him that it was going pretty well. Over a hundred signatures on the online petition so far, according to Ms. Yancey. That was good, but a far cry from what we needed. I mentioned that we were hoping to do a concert in Beaver

Dam to help spread the word. When he asked where we were going to hold it, I admitted we hadn't figured that out yet. "I asked the principal for permission to use the school auditorium, but she said no."

"No surprise there." Everett nodded. "Joyce Fletcher won't do nothin' to bite the hand that feeds her."

"What do you mean?"

"Both wives of them Winter boys sit on the school board. Ain't no way Joyce is gonna do anything that upsets 'em. She's always been scared of them Winters."

This was news to me but helped explain Mrs. Fletcher's attitude about a few things.

"What kinda music you gonna be playin' at this hootenanny? Some of that noisy racket you kids like these days?" There was a little twinkle in his eye, which I took as a possible indication that he was teasing me. But it was hard to tell.

"Actually, it's going to be a wide range of musical genres. We've got the nationally renowned all-female band called Lite Brite hailing from Chicago, Illinois. The musical stylings of the Ward Cleavers from Franklin, North Carolina, who pay a mixture of punk and old-time mountain music."

Everett's eyebrows raised. "That sounds like a match made in hell."

Ignoring him, I continued. "And we also have a local act called the Tucker Trio."

Everett stared at me for a second. "The Tucker Trio? The Tucker Trio are playin' this hoedown?" Everett eyed me dubiously. Grandpop was looking at me closely too.

"Uh, yeah." I looked at them both, slightly confused.

"You didn't mention that to me," Grandpop said.

I thought I had, but I guess I hadn't.

"And how in the Sam Hill did you pull that off?" Everett wanted to know.

"Um, my friend Shawn is their nephew. He asked them and they said yes. Why? What's the big deal?"

"The Tucker Trio are local legends 'round these parts," replied Grandpop.

"Indeed they are. Probably some of the best fiddlin' you've ever heard," Everett said. "I thought they done called it quits for good. You get the Tucker Trio to play and folks'll come out of the woodwork to see 'em."

"Really?" Shawn hadn't mentioned that they were famous, or even local legends.

"Well, I tell you what," said Everett after a moment. "I've got the warehouse out back that's sittin' empty. If you wanna clean it up some, you folks are welcome to use it for your wing-ding."

"Oh my god, that'd be awesome!"

"Well, you should take a look at it first to make sure it'll do. It's kinda run down and needs a good cleanin'. But I'm happy to help. It's for a good cause, but the fact that it'll upset the Winters *and* I'll get to see the Tucker Trio again? Heck, that's just too good to pass up."

I know he was like a hundred years older than me, but at that moment I was pretty sure I was in love with Everett.

I called Ben at Cherryhill and told him about Everett's offer. He said he could come out to Beaver Dam on Thursday afternoon with Betty to check out the warehouse. He offered to meet me at school and give me a ride over to Everett's.

On Monday, I had another present in my locker.

I could smell it before I even got halfway down the hall.

People were holding their noses, the stench was so bad. As soon as I smelled the rank odor, I knew I was the target. I almost gagged when I opened the locker and the dead rat fell out. Several people around me screamed and ran away. Before I knew it, one of the janitors was standing next to me. "How in the world did that get in there?" He looked at me, holding a handkerchief to his face to block the smell. "You didn't bring that thing in, didya?"

I was holding my nose and my eyes had started to run. I wasn't crying, I swear. It's just that the smell of the dead rat made my eyes water. "Of course not! Why would I put a dead rat in my own locker?"

"Kids do all sorts of crazy things these days."

Unsurprisingly, I was sent to the principal's office to discuss the matter. Also unsurprisingly, Mrs. Fletcher tried to blame it on me. "Perhaps you brought your pet rat in on Friday and left it in there over the weekend." Even though she was behind her desk, I was on the edge of my seat in case she jumped up and came at me again.

"First of all, I don't have a pet rat. Second, why would I bring it to school and leave it in my own locker?"

"Well, you do strike me as the forgetful kind." She tilted her head down to look at me from over the edge of her reading glasses.

"It is clear that someone else left it in there. Even a fool can see that!"

She narrowed her eyes. "Watch it, little lady. Don't call me a fool. And unless you have any evidence, I would be careful you don't go around accusing anyone falsely."

I sat back in the chair, crossed my arms and glowered at her. I don't know which I hated more, being called 'little lady,' having someone stick a dead animal in my locker, or getting blamed for it myself. But the combination of the three pushed me over the edge.

"Every time I step into your office, Mrs. Fletcher, I feel like I am entering Crazytown. I'm clearly the target of Bethany's bullying, but you keep trying to pin everything on me."

"Why on earth would Bethany Winter put a dead rat in your locker?"

"Why don't you ask her yourself?" I snapped back.

"I will do no such thing. There is no evidence that she or anyone else is bullying you. Rather, what seems apparent to me is that you are repeatedly acting out in order to get attention. But if you aren't careful, Miss Talcott, it will be detention, not attention, you get. This is your final warning. You may be excused now."

I tried to give her my best why-were-you-born look before I got up and left.

By the time I got to Mrs. Critcher's room, they were already in the middle of class. As I walked to my desk, Bethany made a face that looked like a mouse eating cheese. I guess that was her best imitation of a rat. I would have assumed it came naturally to her.

Of course, Rita and Shawn had heard about the dead rat. Everyone in school heard about it, probably because everyone in school could smell it. But after recounting my conversation with Mrs. Fletcher, Rita responded with the appropriate level of concern and fury. "That's crazy! Did she really think you put it in there yourself?"

"I don't know if she believes it or not. But that seems to be the school's official line."

"Are they gonna give you another locker?"

"I don't know yet. They've still got huge fans trying to air out my locker. The whole hallway smells pretty gross."

"Yeah, it does," Shawn agreed. "I passed there earlier and about puked. Ugh, just thinkin' 'bout it makes me lose my appetite." He set his sandwich down in disgust. I hadn't even bothered opening my lunch because I could still remember the smell.

Rita kept eating the rice dish she had in her Tupperware. "What about all your stuff in there?"

"The books and folders are airing out in front of the fans, but I think I'm going to have to burn my gym clothes."

"Gross!" Rita said, but still not slowing down her eating. Her dedication to her lunch was pretty admirable.

Shawn reached into his backpack and pulled out some papers. "Fortunately, your assignment for Mr. Snead wasn't in there. I was able to proofread it over the weekend." He handed the papers to me. They were covered, and I mean covered, with red ink.

"Holy crudola, was it that bad?"

"Actually, I thought it was really good. You've got some great ideas there. I even learned a few things. But, yeah, there were a lot of writing mistakes. I didn't change anything, just circled your spellin' mistakes with the correct spellings written above. And I underlined grievous grammar mistakes, with a few suggestions on how to correct 'em."

"Oh, wow, Shawn. Thanks so much for doing this. I hope it didn't take too long."

"No biggie. It didn't take long at all." He took a tentative a nibble of a celery stick as he opened up *The Hobbit*. I guess his appetite was returning. But mine definitely wasn't.

Suddenly I remembered that I hadn't updated them on what had transpired over the weekend. I let them know that Everett had offered his warehouse and that the Ward Cleavers had agreed to play. Rita clapped with excitement.

I turned to Rita. "Oh, and Shawn forgot to tell us that his relative's group was super famous."

"They are?" She looked over at Shawn.

"Well, not *famous* famous," he said demurely from behind his book. "But they are fairly well known in certain quarters."

"Everett about had a conniption when I told him the Tucker Trio were performing."

"Really? He was excited?" Shawn looked up from *The Hobbit*.

"Yeah. He said that people would be coming out of the woodwork to see them play. Those were his exact words."

Shawn looked pleased. "That's cool. I'll tell 'em he said that. It'll make 'em feel good. I think they're a bit nervous 'bout playin' again."

"We should have them headline, if they are so famous," I said.

He about jumped out of his seat. "No, that would make 'em really nervous!"

He looked so scared, I couldn't help but laugh. I also told them about Betty's T-shirts and promised to bring theirs in the next day. Without looking at Rita, I added "Betty is giving them to us for free. They're her gifts to us." I didn't want Rita to think that I was patronizing her by paying for them myself. But she didn't say anything, so I assumed everything was cool.

If the shirts had been in my locker that morning, they would have stunk of dead rat. Thinking of that rat stench made me queasy again. I shoved my lunch bag further down into my backpack.

I definitely wouldn't be eating lunch today.

So I was starving when I got off the bus in the afternoon. But as I walked up the driveway, I noticed sticks with orange flags placed all over the yard. Grandpop was standing in the backyard, arms crossed, looking at the orange flags running through his garden. He explained that surveyors had shown up first thing in the morning and started marking out the proposed route for the bypass.

It looked like the Winters were playing hardball.

When I left for school the next morning, I noticed the flags were no longer in the garden. At the top of the driveway, I saw them piled up neatly next to the trash can. I smiled, thinking that Grandpop had probably pulled them all up during the night.

At lunch, I gave Shawn and Rita their Gas Mask Girl T-shirts. They were super excited about how awesome the design looked. But I had to carry the shirts around with me all morning, along with all my books and folders, because my locker still stank like a dead rat. They had the fans running constantly in the hallway, but it was still stinky. At the end of the day, Mrs. Fletcher informed me that she had decided not to give me a new locker. She said that I had to take responsibility for my own actions.

Whatever.

I brought an extra backpack to school the next day in order to carry all my folders and books around with me. The stench in the locker was getting a little bit better, but I was pretty sure anything I left in there for even a few minutes would still smell horrible.

Despite having to carry all of my stuff with me wherever I went, I was excited about going to school because Ben and Betty were picking me up afterwards in order to check out Everett's warehouse space.

I was a bit nervous about meeting Betty. I loved her songs, her singing, and her playing with the Ward Cleavers. She seemed so cool. I didn't want her to think I was some major dweebish dork-butt when we met. So I decided to wear my Gas Mask Girl shirt in order to make a good first impression.

I was walking down the hallway after my Spanish class when I saw another Gas Mask Girl shirt walking toward me. At first I thought it must have been Rita or Shawn. But as I got closer, I realized it was a boy I didn't know well. I had seen him around before, but he'd seemed fairly nondescript, usually wearing long-sleeve flannel shirts, blue jeans, and fashionably scraggly hair.

But here he was walking down the hall with the Gas Mask Girl shirt on. His face broke into a huge grin when he saw me walking toward him in my matching shirt.

"Right on, sister!" he called out. He made a fist in the air and said in a loud voice, "No asphalt plant in Beaver Dam!" Then he gave me a high five as he passed by.

My hand stung a little, and it took me a second to pick my jaw up off the ground and rush off to my next class.

I was buzzing from my encounter with the kid for the rest

of the day. I kept my eyes peeled whenever I was walking in the halls but didn't see him again. There was only one way he could have gotten that shirt, and that was by going to Cherryhill. I don't know why that surprised me. I assumed nobody from school ever went to Franklin. And I had definitely assumed they weren't buying records from Ben. But clearly at least one was.

A little part of me was jealous because I thought Cherryhill was my own special place. But I was also excited that there was another kid shopping at such a cool store. More importantly, they were down with the asphalt plant protest!

I was lost in these thoughts as I walked across the parking lot to meet Ben and Betty when I felt my feet come flying out from underneath me and I tumbled forward. I was holding on to both of my backpacks, full of all my books and folders. I couldn't get my hands up in time to break my fall, but I managed to pitch slightly to the right so that almost all of my weight landed on one of the bags, as opposed to me face-planting. But the bags and folders smashed into my sides, knocking the wind right out of me, and I skidded across the sidewalk. I lay on the ground, gasping for breath. Pain shot through my right knee from where it had hit the pavement. I heard a familiar cackle of laughter behind me.

The Turd-faced Twinkies.

I was still fighting to get my breath back when Bethany leaned down next to me. Her eyes were on fire with hatred. "I've tried being subtle, Vicious Sydney, but you just don't have a clue, do you? So lemme spell it out for you. Don't mess with me, with my family, or with Beaver Dam."

She was leaning next to me, and she placed her knee on top of my right knee. I felt her push down as hard as she could. It probably wasn't that hard, really, and it probably wouldn't have normally hurt. But because I had already damaged my knee in my fall, it really, *really* hurt. It felt like a hundred razors stabbing under my knee cap.

"Crawl back to Rochester, loser."

As she stood up, she put her hand on my side and, with all of her weight, pushed herself up. The pain was excruciating, but I couldn't cry out because I still hadn't caught my breath. Tears were running down my face.

"Or else things are gonna get much worse for you."

Still trying to catch my breath, I rolled over and watched Bethany and her friends walk toward a big black SUV in the parking lot. Her dad was standing next to it, staring at me. Bethany gave him a hug when she got to the vehicle and he kissed the top of her head. The pack of clones got into the back seats, laughing. But one of the twins kept glancing back uncomfortably. As Bradley Winter walked to the driver's side, he continued looking at me expressionlessly.

After a few moments, a couple of kids came over to see if I was okay. The buses had already pulled out of the parking lot. One girl gave me a pack of tissues to dry my tears and blot the blood that was coming from my knee. The knees in my jeans were already ripped, so when I went down, the pavement had cut right through the skin. My knee was covered with bloody strips of skin that had been peeled back, as if someone had used a cheese grater on them.

After I caught my breath and stopped crying, I tried to stand. The tissue girl gave me a hand. My bloodied knee was super sore and couldn't take all of my weight, but it wasn't broken. I pulled up my shirt to check my side and I could see bruises starting to blossom from where I had landed on the books and binders. And from where Bethany had pressed down.

I guess there was blood on my hands when I did that, because now bloodstains were smeared across my T-shirt. My brand-new Gas Mask Girl shirt. Dang it.

Seeing my ruined shirt made me start crying again.

I plopped down on one of my backpacks and just put my head between my knees. I felt exhausted and defeated. I just wanted to melt into the ground and be left alone. I sat like that for what seemed like hours. Crying softly and wishing I could just fade away. I didn't hear my name being called until I felt a hand on my shoulder.

"Sydney? Sydney, are you okay?"

I looked up and Ben was kneeling next to me with a concerned look on his face. "Oh crap, look at your knee. What happened?"

I wiped my eyes. "I fell. Actually, I was tripped. But I'm okay, I think."

"Here, lemme help you up." He put his hand under my arm and lifted me up.

That's when I noticed the woman standing next to him.

She was wearing this amazing vintage purple and black crushed velvet dress, big black army boots, and a Betty Page-style haircut with purple streaks in it.

It was Betty.

And here I was in torn, bloodstained clothes, with tears and snot running down my face. So much for good first impressions.

She looked at me and said "Oh, honey." And then she threw her arms around me and gave me the biggest, longest, greatest hug in the history of hugs.

"What a wretched li'l piece of trash," Betty said.

I was sitting in the back seat of Ben's car. Betty sat next to me, holding my hand. Ben was up front, with his arm draped across the seat. We were still parked in the school lot. He and Betty had walked me over to the car and we'd been sitting there while I told them about my most recent run-in with Bethany Winter, complete with details of past incidents as well.

"And this is the daughter of the guy involved in the asphalt plant, right?" Ben said.

"Yeah. Her dad is Bradley Winter, who is selling the land

for the plant. And he just stood by his car, watching the whole thing happen."

"I know all about the Winter family," Betty said. "I grew up in Beaver Dam. That family's nothing but evil. Well, most of 'em, at least."

"You grew up here?" I looked her in the eye for the first time. I had avoided making eye contact with her out of fear that I'd start crying again. Plus, I was more than a little intimidated by her awesomeness.

"Beaver Dam, born and bred." She smiled at me. Her teeth were a bit wonky, making her both more human and more cool. "I lived here till I moved to the big, bad city of Franklin for college. Been there ever since."

She looked out the window toward the school. "But I went to the old middle school. They hadn't built this one yet. In fact, there wasn't even a Laurel Ridge Road back then." She waved her hand toward the outside. "This is all new to me."

Ben looked at me. "How you doin', Sydney? Do you still wanna see this warehouse or should I take you home?"

"Uh, I'm okay, I guess."

"No rush. You tell me when you're ready."

I looked at Betty, who gave me a smile and a slight squeeze of the hand. My knee still hurt like the dickens, but I was feeling a bit better. It was so comforting being with Ben and Betty.

"Yeah, I'm ready. Let's go over to Everett's and check his place out. But,"—I paused to look over at Betty—"could you guys come to school every day and just hang out with me?"

Betty laughed. "Sorry, sugar. As much as I love you, there's no way I'm a'going back to Beaver Dam Middle School. I'm glad I survived those years, but once is more than enough."

Ben started up the car and put it into gear. He glanced back at me in his rearview mirror. "Don't worry, Sydney. It does get better."

Betty squeezed my hand again. "That it does, my dear. That it does."

When we got to Everett's, my tears had dried and I was pretty much presentable. Except my knee was starting to swell and there were definite bruises on my right side from where I landed. But sitting next to Betty and hearing her and Ben joke with each other on the drive over had raised my spirits massively.

When we walked into Everett's hardware store, the little bell rang out. We couldn't see Everett but we heard him call from the back of the store. "Be right with ya!"

We heard him talking to someone and a few minutes later he emerged from the back with an older man in overalls carrying two buckets of paint. We hung back while Everett rang him up, Ben wandering around the shelves looking at an array of hammers and power tools. As the overalls man left carrying the buckets of paint, I noticed a copy of our zine tucked under his arm. He nodded his greetings to us as he passed, and I nodded back.

"Afternoon, missy." Everett looked down at my blood-stained clothes. He started to say something, changed his mind, and then looked over at Ben and Betty. "I suppose you and your friends wanna check out the warehouse, do you?"

He shook hands with Ben, who introduced himself. But did a double-take when he saw Betty. Betty smiled at him. "How you doin', Mr. Cooper?"

A growing expression of recognition crept across Everett's face. "Elizabeth Black, is that you?"

"Yes, sir, it is. How are you? How's Susie doing?"

"Susie's just fine. Livin' down in Florida with her new baby."

"I've seen the pictures she's posted, but I haven't laid my hands on that li'l biscuit yet."

"Oh, them pictures don't do that baby justice. It's a good

thing she inherited my good looks," Everett said, laughing.

Betty laughed and turned to Ben and me. "I went to school with Mr. Cooper's daughter Susie for the longest time. But I haven't seen her in ages. She went off to college in Charlotte, isn't that right, Mr. Cooper?"

"Yep. Then she went to graduate school down in Florida. She's too busy with her job and that new baby of hers to visit her ol' daddy. So what are you doing here, 'lizabeth? You part of this hootenanny that missy here is puttin' together?"

Betty explained that she and Ben were in one of the bands that'd be playing that night. Everett joked that maybe he'd stick around after the Tucker Trio to check them out. At least, I think it was a joke. What wasn't a joke was the warehouse. An old wooden building with concrete floors, it looked as big as a school gym and Ben estimated it would hold several hundred people. Boxes had been piled up against two of the walls and numerous wooden pallets littered the floor. Otherwise, it was fairly empty.

Ben asked about the legality of holding a concert in the old warehouse. Everett surprised me by saying that he had already mentioned the concert to the fire marshal. The marshal was going to stop by the following week and give him an official permit for hosting the event.

Ben was excited. Downright giddy even. He checked out the electric panel to make sure there would be enough juice to power his PA system and decided that it'd be more than sufficient. He walked around, imagining where he would set up a small stage and the speakers. He pointed to the back of the room. "And we can set up merch tables back here against that wall."

"Merch tables?" Everett said.

"Tables for selling merchandise. The bands can sell T-shirts, records, and whatever else they have. Plus, we can have a couple tables to distribute Sydney's zine and have copies of the petition for people to sign."

"That reminds me," Everett said, turning to me. "I'm gonna need some extra copies of that li'l book-thing of yours, if'n you got some to spare. I just gave Lester my last copy."

"You got it!"

I was battered, bloodied, and bruised, but feeling good about how the day was turning out.

14

"Miss Talcott and Mister Tucker, can I see you both after class, please?" Mr. Snead said as he walked toward his desk. He had just handed out the next assignment, which would require us to do a bit of creative historical fiction.

I wasn't sure why Mr. Snead wanted to talk to me, but past experience suggested it couldn't be for anything good. Then again, he'd asked to see Shawn too, which was confusing. I looked over at Shawn, who shrugged when we made eye contact.

When the bell finally rang, I picked up both of my backpacks and carried them to the front of the classroom and dropped them next to Mr. Snead's desk. My right side was still too bruised and sore to hoist them onto my shoulder, so I had been dragging them around school all day.

I leaned down and tried to adjust the bandage around my right knee. The knee was still swollen and sore. Granny had wrapped it with an ace bandage when I got home. I was wearing baggy jeans so nobody could see I had a bandage on. I didn't want Bethany to have the pleasure of knowing how much she had hurt me. Only Shawn knew because I had told him on the bus ride that morning.

He sidled up next to me in front of Mr. Snead's desk. He looked super-nervous and kept pushing his glasses back up his nose, even when he didn't need to. I could tell that he wasn't usually asked to stay after class. I'd be willing to bet that he'd never seen the inside of Mrs. Fletcher's office. He'd probably never had the pleasure of seeing all her stupid cat posters. Granted, until I'd gotten to Beaver Dam, I'd never been sent to a principal's office either.

Mr. Snead, dressed in his usual sweater vest, sat down at his desk and started shuffling through papers. When he found what he was looking for, he held it up for us to see. It was my recent Shakespeare assignment

"I wanted to talk to you two about this. Is there anything either of you want to tell me about this piece of work?" He eyed each of us coolly.

"Um, that's my paper I turned in earlier this week," I said, slightly confused.

"Have you seen this paper before, Mister Tucker?"

Shawn looked like he might faint, but he leaned forward to look closer at the paper in Mr. Snead's hand. "Not that version of it, no."

Mr. Snead set down the paper and clasped his hands atop his desk. "And what exactly do you mean by 'this version'?"

"What Shawn means—" But Mr. Snead cut me off by holding up a hand to hush me. Man, I hate it when people do that to me.

"I'm talking to Mister Tucker right now." He looked at Shawn. "Well?"

"What I mean, sir, is that I saw an earlier version of Sydney's paper. I helped her with all the typos and spellin' mistakes."

"I assume you had your work cut out for you," said Mr. Snead.

"Oh yeah." Shawn laughed. "You have no idea."

"Hey! I'm standing right here!"

Mr. Snead raised his hand to hush me again. That hand-thing was getting on my nerves. I'm sure Joan Jett would have broken it off, but I felt it best to squelch that impulse.

"Actually, I do have an idea," Mr. Snead was saying. "I also have an idea that you did more than correct her spelling mistakes. Isn't that right, Mister Tucker?"

I started to respond, but Shawn beat me to it. He looked like Mr. Snead had slapped him. "Absolutely not, Mr. Snead!

All I did was circle her spellin' mistakes and underline a few grammar errors. I told her the correct spelling for some of the words, but that's it."

"You didn't write any of this paper for her? You didn't perhaps tell her what to write and how to write it?"

"He did not!" I was fuming. Mr. Snead held up his hand again, but I continued. "Are you accusing me of cheating? I wrote that paper myself. Shawn just helped me with my cruddy spelling and grammar. But all of those ideas are my own!"

"It's true, sir." Shawn was looking seriously at Mr. Snead. "I just helped out by proofreadin' her paper. But I was impressed by how good her paper was. Sydney is really smart, if you can get past her atrocious spellin'."

"Still standing right here!"

Mr. Snead leaned back in his chair and kept looking back and forth between Shawn and me. He was silent for at least thirty seconds, but it felt like an hour. I stared at him angrily. I didn't like being accused of cheating just because he thought I wasn't smart.

He looked to Shawn. "Mister Tucker, you are certain that you did no more than proofread Miss Talcott's paper?"

"Yes, sir. I swear to it."

That seemed enough to convince Mr. Snead of Shawn's innocence. He then turned to me. "And you, Miss Talcott? Do you swear that nobody else helped you write this paper? Besides Mister Tucker's proofreading assistance, this work is all your own?"

"Yes, I wrote the whole thing myself. I know you two enjoy making fun of my spelling, but I'm not stupid! I'm just as smart as anyone else in this school."

Mr. Snead cocked an eyebrow.

"Well, I may not be as brilliant as Shawn, but I'm pretty smart myself."

"Yes, I guess you are." Mr. Snead handed me the paper.

"This is very good work."

You could have knocked me down with a sneeze. I wasn't expecting that at all.

Taking the paper from him, I flipped to the back page. There was a full paragraph of comments, but I couldn't focus on them. I was too distracted by the A+ grade at the bottom of the page.

"As you can see," Mr. Snead was saying. "I take issue with some of your conclusions. But you've got a number of insightful ideas that are quite impressive. I usually see that level of analysis from only one other student in this class." He tilted his head toward Shawn, who flinched at the praise. "So one might understand why I drew the conclusion that I did."

"But you've now set the bar fairly high, Miss Talcott," he continued. "I'm expecting you to continue meeting it. Do you understand?"

"Er, yes, sir."

"All right, you two can go on to your next class."

I was already halfway out the door when an idea hit me. I turned around at the threshold. "Um, Mr. Snead?"

Shawn, who had already walked out into the hall, turned around with a look of confusion on his face. Mr. Snead peered up from his desk.

"Yes, Miss Talcott? Is there anything else?"

"You are a musician, right?"

"Um, yes, I am. Does that have anything to do with anything?"

"Would you like to play at a benefit concert?" Mr. Snead looked stunned. I felt a twinge of enjoyment for making him speechless. "You know that petition drive about the asphalt plant that you helped us post online? Well, Shawn, Rita, and I are organizing a concert to help raise awareness and promote the referendum. We'd love to have you participate."

Mr. Snead just blinked. I swear, I could smell his mind melting.

But maybe that was just the lingering dead rat smell.

"It's a diverse and eclectic line-up featuring Lite Brite, the Ward Cleavers, and the Tucker Trio," I added.

Mr. Snead, finding his voice, stammered, "You want me to play a concert? With the Tucker Trio?"

"Well, you wouldn't be playing *with* them. You'd open the show. Maybe play for twenty to thirty minutes. What do you think?"

"Um, let me think about it."

He still looked a bit stunned when I turned to leave.

But I knew he was going to say yes.

Of course Mr. Snead agreed to play. He said a few friends would join him and they'd play some bluegrass tunes.

"But we don't have a name yet," he said when Shawn and I approached him a few days later.

I thought for a second and was about to suggest they just list their last names, when Shawn piped up, "How about 'Bluegrass Lawnmower'?"

I looked at him in disbelief. "Shawn, that's a brilliant name."

Shawn smiled self-consciously. "Yeah, I know."

Later at lunch I asked him where he came up with the name.

"It's one of the many names I've considered if I ever have a band."

Rita had just taken a sip from her water bottle and started to choke on it.

"Dude, you should totally form a band!" I exclaimed, while slapping Rita on the back. I still couldn't imagine seeing Shawn rocking out on a stage, but I'd definitely pay good money for the opportunity. "But now you've given your name away."

"Oh, I've got lots of names that are better'n that one." He smiled deviously before putting his head back behind a book.

After a few seconds, I could hear the crunch of a carrot.

A few days later I got a letter from Dani. It was a single page, written in all caps, with each sentence taking up several lines.

DEAR SYDNEY!

WE ARE SO IN!! WE CAN'T WAIT TO SEE YOU AND WE'RE SUPER STOKED TO PLAY THE CONCERT IN BEAVER DAM. WOO HOO!!!! GOTTA RUN, BUT WILL WRITE MORE LATER. XOX-OXO DANI

Of course, she still took the time to draw a little self-portrait of herself smiling hugely and holding a sign that said "Beaver Dam or Bust!"

The next several weeks were a blur as we got ready for the concert. We made posters using Betty's Gas Mask Girl image and put them up throughout Beaver Dam. Ben and Betty took some to put up in Franklin and on the university campus. Every few days, I had to go around Beaver Dam to replace the ones that would inevitably get torn down.

Every few days someone from the county came out and put new orange flags in Granny and Grandpop's yard, marking where the proposed bypass would go. During the night, Grandpop would pull them up and stack them neatly next to the trash can. Neither he nor Granny ever said a word about it, so I kept my mouth shut as well.

A few more kids were wearing Gas Mask Girl T-shirts around school. I spotted five or six different students wearing them during those weeks before the show. I worked hard to avoid Bethany at school. I didn't bother using my locker anymore, assuming that it was too easy a target. Of course that meant that I had to carry everything around in two backpacks. But I was getting used to it, and probably getting a little more buff from the workout.

I always made sure I walked near other people when I was going to and from the bus. I wasn't being paranoid. I just assumed that, with the momentum building toward the concert, Bethany would try to lash out at me.

I was right.

I just hadn't anticipated how nasty she would be when she did strike.

It was a Monday when I walked into the library for lunch to find Mrs. Fletcher standing behind the desk next to an older man dressed in a tired-looking tweed jacket, complete with leather patches on the elbows and a poorly tied bow tie. Imagine your worst stereotype of an old male librarian, and you'd be halfway there. Rita and Shawn were standing in front of the desk with their coats and backpacks still on.

I had a bad feeling about things.

I looked around. "Where's Ms. Yancey?"

Mrs. Fletcher looked over her reading glasses at me. "I was just telling your friends that Ms. Yancey will no longer be working in our library."

Rita's face was radiating anger, while Shawn looked like he was in a stupor.

"They fired her," Rita exclaimed.

"What? Why?" I turned toward Mrs. Fletcher, my fists clenched involuntarily.

She sniffed about as patronizing a sniff as one could possibly sniff. "Ms. Yancey's employment at Beaver Dam has been terminated. It has come to my attention that she has been using school resources for unauthorized activities."

"And what is that supposed to mean?"

"It means that she was using school computers to engage in unauthorized political activities." She eyed me closely. "You wouldn't know anything about that, now would you, Miss Talcott?"

And that's when it hit me. She had fired Ms. Yancey for helping me research the asphalt plant, HD Dunkirk Industries, and its ties to the Winter family. Ms. Yancey had known that they might check the computer records and she had protected me by having me use her own account. And she had paid the price by losing her job.

"I have no idea what you're talking about." I used my most honest-sounding voice, but nobody in earshot was convinced.

"That's what I thought you'd say." Mrs. Fletcher gestured to the man standing quietly behind her. "This is Mr. Richardson, our new librarian. In addition to taking over the library, he will also be enforcing our rules a bit more *rigorously* than did Ms. Yancey."

Shawn, Rita, and I exchanged glances with a sense of dread.

"For one thing, students are able to check out only two books at a time. Looking over the records here," said Mrs. Fletcher, glancing down at some papers she had in front of her, "you have all greatly abused the system. For instance, Mr. Tucker, it seems you have well over two dozen books currently checked out."

Shawn started to speak, but Mrs. Fletcher cut him off. "All of your books are due on Friday. No exceptions."

Before we could protest, Mrs. Fletcher pressed on. "And secondly, students are clearly not allowed to bring food into the library. I've been informed that Ms. Yancey was extremely lax about enforcing this important rule with you three. Well, those days are over."

"But—" Rita stammered, but Mrs. Fletcher held her hand up to cut Rita off. I was familiar with this hushing-hand routine. I just glowered at Mrs. Fletcher. I knew this was not a battle we were going to win.

"No buts, Miss Gonzalez. This is a library, not a restaurant. If you want to eat lunch, you will do it in the cafeteria with all the other students. You three need to be reminded that you do not get special treatment. Mr. Richardson is under strict orders to make sure there is no eating in the library. Anyone caught with food will be banned from the library. Isn't that right, Mr. Richardson?"

Mr. Richardson, who had been standing quietly by the principal's side, jumped slightly at the sound of his name. "What was that? Oh yes. Absolutely no eating in the library. No food at all, no, no, no…" he muttered, trailing off.

"Now." Mrs. Fletcher waved her hands at us, as if she were brushing us out of the door. "You three go down to the cafeteria and eat your lunch. You aren't allowed back in here until you return all the books you currently have checked out."

As we walked out of the library, I heard a familiar cackle. Bethany was standing in the hallway with three of her piranhas. I noticed that one of the twin sisters was missing. "Ah, what's wrong, losers? Didya get kicked out of your Fortress of Nerditude?"

"Shut up, Bethany." I was so angry I didn't know what I might do, but I did know that Mrs. Fletcher was just a few feet away and that if anything happened with Bethany, I'd get blamed for it.

Bethany knew that too, which is why she seemed bent on provoking me. She stepped closer. "Did your little loser librarian friend get fired? That's just so sad," she cooed in a sing-song voice. The Three Stooges chortled behind her.

"C'mon." I turned toward Rita and Shawn. "Let's get out of here."

"Ah, but where are you gonna go? You've lost your little clubhouse. No more lunchtime playdates for plotting and scheming."

Shawn tugged my arm to encourage me to walk away. But before I could move, Rita stepped in between Bethany and me. She was inches away from Bethany's face when she unleashed a flurry of Spanish. I'm not sure exactly what Rita said, but I could tell it wasn't pretty. I think I recognized a few Spanish words for body parts. And I'm fairly certain there were more curse words in that twenty-second outburst than I could possibly count.

When she finished, Rita turned around, grabbed mine and Shawn's arms, and walked toward the end of the hallway. Bethany had looked stunned the whole time Rita had been in her face. But now that we were a safe distance away, we heard Bethany shout out, "Speak English, loser!"

Without turning around or breaking our stride, Rita and I both raised our right hands in the air and gave her the one-finger salute.

Dear Sydney!

Hello from the beginning of our tour. We played in Columbus, Ohio last night and it was pretty great. We're trying out a bunch of our new songs and they seem to be going well. We played with some old friends in the band Lemuria, who are super sweet. We're on the road for the next several weeks, but all we're talking about is getting to visit you in Beaver Dam. We appreciate you and your grandparents being able to put us up for the night. I hope that isn't gonna be a problem. I can't wait to see the farm you live on. And we're super psyched to play the benefit show. I hope we get a good crowd for your sake, but we're just stoked to play! And I'm also stoked to be playing with the Ward Cleavers. We've been listening to their album on the drive this morning. Everyone loves it. But I'm the most stokedest (new word!) to get to hang out with YOU! I can't wait!! See you in less than two weeks!!!

xoxo DANI

At the bottom of the letter was a drawing of a van with Dani hanging out of the window and waving.

The week before the concert, Betty and Ben agreed to help me clean out Everett's warehouse space. They picked me up from school again. But this time I waited inside the entrance until I saw Ben's car pull into the parking lot. I wasn't scared of Bethany or anything like that. It's just that my sense of self-preservation was strong enough to convince me that I should play it safe.

When we got to the warehouse, Ben borrowed a huge ladder from Everett and went around replacing all the light bulbs in the building and setting up a few spotlights for the stage. Betty and I started sweeping and mopping the entire floor.

I was still in awe of Betty's coolness. She showed up wearing faded overalls and bright-yellow Converse hi-tops. But, despite feeling intimidated, it was so easy to talk with her. Noting the old Pixies T-shirt that she was wearing underneath her overalls, I mentioned how much I liked their original bass player, Kim Deal.

"Oh, my gosh, Kim Deal is so cool!" Betty exclaimed. "I especially dig The Breeders. Have you ever listened to them?"

"I love The Breeders so much! The way she harmonizes with her sister is just amazing."

"I know! I wish I had a sister just so I could sing with someone like that. What's your favorite Breeders song?"

It went on like that for most of the afternoon. She would ask me questions and listen to my answers. We shared so many interests. She was like Kris, except two decades older. And if I'm being honest, Kris was never as good a listener as Betty. Nobody listened to me like this.

Well, except maybe Rita. I'd never thought much about it before, but Rita was an attentive listener and she always asked me lots of good questions. We didn't share musical interests the way Betty and I did. But I had to admit that Rita was pretty much aces.

I swept the warehouse floor with a broom and dustpan, while Betty followed behind me with her mop and bucket. The floor was so filthy we had to stop every few minutes to empty the dustpan and change the mop water in the bucket.

After a few minutes, our conversation turned to the topic of friends.

"There were a few people in school that I was on friendly terms with," Betty said. "But I didn't have any *close* friends. Nobody really got me, ya know? It wasn't till I went to college that I found folks who thought like me and were into the things that I was into."

"Yeah, back in Rochester I had a really close friend named Kris. We hung out together all the time and were into the same stuff. She also loved Kim Deal."

"That's cool. Do you stay in touch with her much?"

"A little…Well, not really. Her letters are getting pretty rare. She seems to be hanging out with a new group of friends. Plus, she's got a *boyfriend* now." I mimed the universal sign for barfing.

Betty laughed. "Well, sugar, that happens, I gotta tell ya. Datin' can change the situation. Hopefully your friendship is strong enough to survive things like that."

"Yeah. It used to bother me more than it does now." And as I said that, I realized it was true. I hadn't been upset about Kris and her lack of letters for weeks because I had so much other stuff going on myself. I had been worried that she was moving on, when it turned out I was doing the same thing. As I went to dump yet another dustpan of dirt in the garbage can, I added, "I've got two good friends in Beaver Dam, Shawn and Rita."

"That's great. You're so lucky."

"Yeah, they're not really into music or other stuff I'm into, except for reading. But they get me. Plus, they're pretty awesome in their own way." And as I said that, I knew it was true too.

"I've never asked if you play any instruments," Betty asked casually as she swirled the mop across the floor.

"My dad tried to teach me when I was younger, but it just seemed to be beyond me."

Betty laughed. "Is he a musician?"

"He was. When he was younger he had a few near-misses with success. But when he got older he was just playing in cheesy rock-n-roll cover bands that mostly played bar shows and wedding receptions. They were all okay, but none of them great or memorable. Mom and Dad were always fighting about it. He refused to quit and settle down. It drove my mom crazy."

"Is that why they divorced?" Betty asked.

I felt my chest tighten. "They never divorced. Dad was killed two years ago."

Betty stopped mopping and looked up. "Oh, baby, I'm sorry. I shouldn't have assumed anything."

"It's okay. I don't really talk about it much."

Or ever, I thought to myself. But when I looked up at Betty, the love and concern in her eyes pierced right through my heart.

My voice quaked as I continued. "A couple of years ago, a drunk driver plowed into Dad's car as he was on his way home from a gig. He and his drummer were killed instantly. They say the drunk driver walked away from the wreck without a scratch."

"Oh, Sydney, that must have been horrible for you."

I could feel the tears trickling down my cheek.

"Yeah, it was rough. But I know it was worse on Mom. They had been fighting before he left. It was Thanksgiving weekend and she was mad that he wasn't spending it with the family. She said some pretty hateful things before he left. And then he was gone. She went to a really dark place afterwards. It was…it was…" My voice caught and the tears rolled freely down my face. "It was like losing both parents at once."

"Oh, sugar. I'm so sorry. I had no idea." Betty let the mop drop to the floor and wrapped her arms around me. "Baby, I'm so sorry." In her warm embrace, I just melted, crying into her shoulder.

I don't know how long we stayed like that. I'd finally gotten my tears under control, but Betty didn't stop hugging me until we heard the door open behind us.

Betty and I had been so wrapped up in our earlier conversation, I hadn't noticed that Ben had disappeared. Now he was standing there with Everett, looking worried.

"Um, Everett has some bad news, y'all."

"What's up, Mr. Cooper?" Betty said, finally breaking her embrace and leaning over to pick up the mop she had dropped. I wiped my face with the sleeve of my shirt. Ben and Everett didn't appear to notice I had been crying.

"Well, it seems that the fire marshal ain't too sure this hootenanny can go ahead after all." Everett was holding an official-looking letter.

My stomach dropped. "What? I thought they'd already given you their approval."

"That they did. But it now seems 'new information has come to their attention,'" he said, reading from the letter. "They say they need to do a fuller inspection of the entire premises."

Betty plopped the mop back into the bucket filled with black water, wiped her hands on her overalls, and reached out for the letter. "That shouldn't be a problem, should it?"

"That ain't all." Everett handed Betty the letter. "It says that we need to apply for an 'event permit.'"

"What's that supposed to mean?" I was starting to panic.

"Ain't never heard of one before. Probably some bureaucratic red tape. But if you was to ask me, I'd say someone is pressuring them to shut this thing down."

Betty looked up from the letter and glanced around at the rest of us. "Who? Why?"

"The Winters are behind this, I just know it."

I felt my cheeks burning as the anger rose inside me.

Why did everything have to be such a struggle? Sensing my fragility, Betty stepped over and put her hand on my shoulder.

"What are we gonna do?" Ben asked, looking at Everett, who seemed to be the best person to answer the question.

"Well, it's 'bout 4:15 now." Everett looked down at his watch. "I 'spect them boys at the fire marshal's office are still there. What say we go and ask 'em?"

Ben, Betty, and I piled into Ben's car and followed Everett's truck to the county offices. When we walked into the fire marshal's office, everyone seemed to know Everett but were a little taken aback to see all of us walking in with him. The fire marshal came out of his office and shook all of our hands. He was an older man, probably Everett's age, and he seemed to know why we were there before we even said anything. He asked Everett if he would mind stepping into his office alone for a few minutes. They disappeared into the back, leaving the rest of us standing by the front counter.

Betty turned to me and winked. Without even bothering to lower her voice she said, "See, honey, this is how the patriarchy works. You want somethin' done, sometimes you've gotta work through the old boys' network. Those are the privileges that come with male genitalia. Ain't that right, Benjamin?"

Ben chuckled. "That seems to be the case, don't it?"

Betty continued speaking to me. "Know what you're up against, my dear. It's a lifelong struggle."

After another minute or two, the office door opened and Everett walked out. He turned back to the fire marshal and shook his hand. As Everett walked toward us, he gave us a quick nod and headed toward the door. We took his cue and silently followed him out.

No one spoke until we got to the parking lot. Everett

leaned up against the door of his battered truck and crossed his arms. "Well, it looks like we was right. The marshal is gettin' pressure from the Winter boys to make sure this thing don't happen."

"So they're gonna shut us down?" I felt the little bit of optimism that had been creeping back in quickly drain away.

"Now I didn't say that, did I?" Everett smiled at me. "Them Winters may think they run this town, but the truth is most folk can't stand 'em. Take Jimmy back there." He gestured back toward the county offices. "The county commission are makin' his office reinspect my building and requirin' that we apply for an expensive event permit. But he's gonna come inspect the building himself, so I don't think that'll be too much of a problem."

"What about the event permit? How do we do that?"

"And what do you mean by expensive?" Ben added.

"I already done filled out the application just now. As for the cost, it's gonna be 750 dollars."

"Holy crudola! We don't have that." I turned to look at Ben imploringly.

"I'm sorry, Sydney. But I don't have that much money either."

"Well now," interrupted Everett. "You might not have it now, missy. But that don't mean you ain't gonna have it eventually. You're gonna be sellin' tickets for this wing-ding, ain't ya?"

"Uh, yeah. Five dollars per person."

"Well, then y'all only need to sell 150 tickets to cover the cost, right?"

"But most of the money was gonna go to the bands. Whatever was left over was for the referendum campaign."

Ben spoke up. "The bands'll play for free, I'm sure. That ain't an issue." Betty was nodding her head in agreement. "And I guess this is exactly what that war chest is for."

"But we're only selling tickets at the door, so we won't

have any money until *after* the show. They want the 750 dollars now, right?"

"That they do," Everett said.

"So how are we gonna pay for the permit?"

Everett smiled at me again and got into his truck. "It's already paid for. Don't worry, missy. I know y'all will be able to pay me back. You're good for it."

Betty put her arm around my shoulders and gave me a squeeze as we watched Everett drive away. "And in that life-long struggle, my dear, it's good to know who your allies are."

15

I was so worried about the show—that no one would show up, that those who did would hate the bands, that it'd all be a big flop—that I paced around the house with nervous energy until Granny's nerves couldn't take it anymore. To get me out of Granny's hair, Grandpop offered to drive me to the warehouse, suggesting that we could help with some last-minute prep. So I arrived at the warehouse several hours before the concert was scheduled to start.

All week the weather forecasters had been predicting a rainstorm and, unfortunately, this time they were correct. The rain was coming down in sheets.

Earlier in the day Dani had called from the road. I wasn't in the house, but Granny took the message. The rain was slowing their progress and they said they'd just meet me at the warehouse. According to Granny, Dani also said they had to make a slight detour on their way up the mountain. So in addition to the weather and the attendance, I now had to worry about whether Lite Brite would even get to Beaver Dam in time for the show.

When Grandpop and I got to the warehouse, Ben, Betty, and the rest of the Ward Cleavers were already there. Ben was onstage setting up the PA and running cables everywhere. Betty was helping their drummer set up the drum kit.

"Hey, Sydney, you wanna give us a hand?"

I was happy to have an outlet for my nervous energy, but I told Betty I didn't know anything about how to set drums up.

"It's easy. I'll show you all you need to know." She then proceeded to point out the various drums—snare, bass, floor tom, rack toms—and the cymbals—crash, ride, and high hat—and explained where it all went. Then I helped her set up the microphone stands. Betty explained that since only the Ward Cleavers and Lite Brite were using drums, they were going to share the kit.

"We're also gonna set up a basic backline for everyone to use," Ben added, walking by with an armful of microphone cables.

"What does that mean?" I asked, worrying I sounded too much like a rookie.

Ben knelt down next to the bass drum to set up a microphone in front of it. "A backline is the amplifiers that all the bands will use. I've got several guitar amps and a bass amp as well. So if anyone needs to have their instrument amplified, from a guitar to a banjo, they can just plug into one of the amps and we can adjust the sound accordingly. It saves a lot of time, as opposed to every band settin' up all of their amps and then takin' 'em all down after they play. A shared backline is the best way to go when you've got multiple bands playin' together."

I was about to ask which instruments needed to be amplified when I heard a familiar voice calling out behind me.

"Hey, kiddo!"

I spun around and saw Joey walking across the warehouse floor. "This place looks awesome."

"Joey!" I ran at him as fast as I could. I hadn't seen my brother since December and had been assuming it'd be several more months before I saw him again. He laughed as I catapulted myself into his arms and gave him a huge bear hug.

"What are you doing here?"

He gave me a big squeeze and set me down. "I heard that this was the concert of the century. There was no way I could miss that!"

"But how did you get here?" I couldn't believe he was standing in front of me. I leaned into him for another hug.

"I flew into Charlotte. Lite Brite picked me up and drove

me into town. Dani and I arranged it a few weeks ago." He
shook his hands in the air. "Surprise!"

I looked behind him, but there was no one else there. "Are
they here now?"

"Yeah, they were just waiting a few minutes to see if the
rain would let up before they carried their instruments in."

Just then Dani walked around the corner. She carried a
bass guitar case in one hand and a big bag overflowing with
T-shirts in the other. Her bright-green hair matched the
frames of her star-shaped glasses. She wore a green cardigan
atop a Bikini Kill T-shirt, faded black jeans, and a pair of
Converse hi-tops. Of course, they were green too.

I didn't know if I should play it cool or scream like the
fan-girl that I was. But before I could make up my mind,
Dani decided for me. When she saw me hugging on Joey, she
dropped her guitar case and bag. "Sydney!" she shouted and
started running toward me with her arms open. So I did the
same. We met halfway and gave each other a huge hug.

I about died.

The rest of Lite Brite followed behind her, shaking off
the rain. Ben, Betty, and the other Cleavers walked over to
greet them.

I introduced the people that I knew, and the ones I didn't
introduced themselves. Ben told Lite Brite what a big fan he
was of theirs, and they responded by saying how much they
liked the Ward Cleavers album they'd been listening to in the
van. It was cool to watch instant friendships blossom right in
front of my eyes.

Ben gestured to the stage. "We've almost got everything
set up. Give me five more minutes and y'all can do a sound
check."

Lite Brite said they still needed to bring in a few more
pieces of gear and merchandise. I went out to help them
carry stuff in from the van. If anything, the rain had gotten
worse. It was coming down in buckets.

"Oh no," I said, standing in the doorway, a feeling of dread taking hold in my stomach. "No one is going to come out in this mess."

Dani was standing next to me and looking at the sky. "It'll be fine. How many tickets have you sold already?"

"That's the problem. We didn't sell any in advance. Tickets are only available at the door. And people would be crazy to brave this storm."

"No worries." She gave me a big smile. "We'll be happy to play for everyone who is here now. We don't need a big crowd to have a good time."

"But we *do* need a big crowd. We need to sell at least 150 tickets to cover the cost of the event permit." I explained the issue with the county's event fee to her, as well as a few of the challenges we'd had trying to get the show authorized.

She just gave me another big smile. "Well, worrying about it isn't gonna do a bit of good, so you can stop wasting your energy fretting. You've put a lot of love and energy into this, Sydney. And I've got a good feeling about it." She gave me a sideways hug. "Now what do you say we get ourselves soaking wet?" And she rushed out, laughing, into the pouring rain to get another box out of the van. Her optimism was infectious. I ran after her screaming as the cold rain pelted down on me.

The doors were supposed to open at eight p.m., with the first band advertised to start at eight-thirty. Five minutes before the doors opened, all of the performers had arrived. Lite Brite and the Ward Cleavers were walking around talking amongst themselves. The Tucker Trio had shown up during Lite Brite's sound check and they were in a corner, tuning their instruments and joking around. They were older than I had expected, two of them with healthy doses of gray in their hair. Shawn was there with about a half dozen of his relatives. He told me his uncles and aunt were nervous because they hadn't played live in front of people in over a decade.

But they couldn't have been as nervous as Mr. Snead.

He'd walked in a few minutes before, looking green and drenched from the rain. He'd been so anxious that he hadn't even introduced the rest of his group, two women and another guy. Under their raincoats, they all wore matching light-blue shirts and dark-gray pants. They stood by the side of the stage, also fiddling with their instruments and looking anxious.

Ten minutes after the doors opened, these were the same people in the room. No one else had shown up. Except Everett, who was standing in the back of the room with Grandpop, taking it all in with a bemused look on his face. I was starting to feel lousy about the lack of people.

Ten minutes later, Rita arrived with Sophia, an older sister who had agreed to sell tickets at the door. After she apologized for being late because of the rain, I gestured to the near empty room and said, "No big deal. Look at this place. There's not been a single person to sell a ticket to. The whole thing looks like a real bust."

I could feel my voice crack a little. I felt like a failure. I was so ashamed that people I cared about had taken the time to be here. I had talked Shawn and Rita into believing that we could hold a concert in Beaver Dam. Ben and Betty had done so much to put this show on. Lite Brite had driven far out of their way just to be here. Shawn had talked his nervous relatives into coming out of retirement to play.

And there was no one here. I had let everyone down.

As if sensing my fragile state, Rita put her arm around me and gave me a hug. Shawn strolled up behind her. I was about to apologize to both of them for disappointing them with my stupid concert idea when I heard Dani's voice. "You two must be Shawn and Rita."

Shawn jumped a few inches and Rita looked stunned that someone knew her name.

"I'm Dani. I've heard so much about you both from Sydney. She's told me how lucky she is to have such great friends." Dani shook hands with both of them and I felt my toes tingle with pride. "And let me just say how awesome you three are for fighting against this asphalt plant. You're doing great work. Thanks so much for putting all of this together and inviting us to play. It's an honor to be here." She leaned over and gave me another sideways hug.

I swear, hugs were the only thing keeping me going at that point.

"Uh, thanks," Rita said. "It's nice to meet you too. Sydney has said a lot about you. I'm looking forward to hearing you play. I've been listening to your music all week."

I turned to her. "Really?"

She smiled, a little embarrassed. "Yeah. I know how much you love them, so I figured I should get to know them better."

I gave her a huge smile. That was pretty awesome for a friend to do. Yeah, Rita's a keeper, for sure.

Rita turned back to Dani. "I really like 'The Unbearable Lightness of Being a Girl' song. It's super catchy."

"Aw, thanks, Rita. That's kind of you to say."

"It inspired me to read a couple of Milan Kundera novels," Rita said, and then made a sour face. "I can't say I enjoyed them. But I like your song a lot."

Man, I really should have found out what that song was about before I wrote that essay for Mr. Snead.

It was showtime and we only had about thirty people in the warehouse. More than half of them were the musicians, their friends, and families. Rita went to check on Sophia, who confirmed that she had sold only a dozen tickets so far.

Mr. Snead walked over to ask if we were ready for his group to start.

"Um, there's not many people here. Don't you want to wait until a few more show up?"

"Actually, we're ready to play now. Get it over with, you know." He gave me a strained smile. I think that was the first time I'd ever seen him smile at me.

It suddenly struck me that I'd asked him to play without ever having heard him. For all I knew, he could have been an awful musician. Maybe it was best to have his group play when there weren't that many people in the audience.

I walked up onto the stage to introduce him. When I got to the microphone, there was some polite applause. I heard two female voices hooting and calling out my name. It was Dani and Betty, who were standing together in the middle of the room. I took out a damp, folded piece of paper from my back pocket. I'd known I'd be super nervous doing the introductions, so I had written down what I wanted to say. I read my little speech about the dangers posed by the asphalt plant and the horrible environmental record of HD Dunkirk Industries. I had been tempted to say something about the Winter family and all the challenges they had thrown our way, but both Rita and Shawn advised against it. So instead, I encouraged everyone to sign the petition and take some of the informational material that we had set up at the back of the room. But I was pretty sure that most of the people in attendance had probably signed the petition ages ago.

Just before I announced Mr. Snead, I heard a woman scream. I covered my eyes from the glare of the stage lights and looked out into the room. In the center, my mom was hugging Joey. I guess she'd just arrived and hadn't known that he was coming either.

"Hi, Mom," I called out. "Joey's here!" Which got a laugh from the small audience.

"And without any further ado," I said, putting the speech back into my pocket. "It is my pleasure to introduce my English teacher." Someone hooted in the crowd. I was pretty sure it was Shawn. "Mr. Snead and his band, The Bluegrass Lawnmower!"

There was some spirited applause as the four of them took to the stage. I went to stand by Shawn and Rita with my fingers crossed. If I was worried about how good they were going to be, I needn't have been.

They were amazing. In between songs, they spoke little, with Mr. Snead only introducing the name of the next song. But they tore it up, playing some gorgeous bluegrass.

In each song, they all took turns doing a little solo, which I guess is standard in bluegrass. The tallest of the two women sang and played acoustic guitar, while the other harmonized and played a fiddle. The other guy played an upright bass that he would occasionally spin around with a flourish. But the star was clearly Mr. Snead, who played a different instrument for each song, from mandolin to banjo to some instruments I didn't even know the names of. And he played them all incredibly well. By the end of the second song, most of the crowd had moved to the front of the stage, with the Tucker Trio right up front.

When Mr. Snead introduced the last song of their set, he thanked Shawn and me for inviting them to play, and then said a few strong words about the importance of protecting our shared mountain heritage and how dangerous the proposed asphalt plant was. It was nice to get the shout-out, but I appreciated the forceful attack on the asphalt plant even more.

After Bluegrass Lawnmower left the stage, I saw the Tucker Trio shaking hands with Mr. Snead and his group. They were all beaming from the praise and attention. I don't think I'd ever seen Mr. Snead so happy, and he was definitely more relaxed now that his set was over. The lights came up and I looked around the room, but only about a dozen more people had shown up. The warehouse was still almost completely empty. The music had lifted my spirits, but now I felt my stomach tighten again with the realization that the show was turning out to be a complete bust.

The Ward Cleavers started plugging in their instruments. Ben walked up to the microphone to check the levels and I suddenly wondered who was running the PA, since he and Betty were onstage. I turned around to see Dani behind the board, adjusting the levels. She smiled and waved me over.

"What do you know about running sound, Sydney?"

"Uh, absolutely nothing."

"Well, stand next to me and I'll show you how it's done." She winked at me. "The best soundmen are women, and don't let anyone ever tell you otherwise."

So during the Ward Cleavers set, Dani showed me how the soundboard worked. She showed me how to set the gain knobs to avoid getting feedback. How to set the faders for each channel in order to get the best mix. How to make a different mix for the monitors onstage so that the band could hear themselves clearly.

When the Ward Cleavers started, they launched into one of their more rockin' songs. They were far louder than Mr. Snead's band had been, and everyone took several steps backward when the music hit them. There weren't too many people standing in front of the stage. Except Shawn, who seemed like his shoes were glued to the floor. He had a look of pure amazement on his face and seemed especially in awe of Betty's playing.

What I had heard on their record was a cool blend of punk and what I had considered bluegrass. But Ben had informed me that there was a difference between bluegrass and old-time mountain music, and that they took their inspiration from the latter. And after their first song, their mountain roots became much more obvious to me. Betty was front and center with her fiddle, and the music, though still fast and loud, definitely had a twang to it.

When they ended their first song, the other members of

Lite Brite were dancing in front of the stage. But by the time the second song finished, they'd been joined by a growing group of fans, with Shawn still rooted in place. One of the people dancing around looked a lot like one of the twins that hung around Bethany, but since she was all alone, I decided it couldn't be her.

For the third song, Betty stepped up to the microphone.

"Hey, y'all. Thanks for comin' out. This next song is called 'Mountain Laurel.' It's about the natural beauty of our environment and how it is up to us to protect that beauty. We're here to make sure HD Dunkirk and their friends don't build an asphalt plant right here in my hometown of Beaver Dam, right next to the school. We're here to take a stand against those who destroy our mountains with their greed. We're here to fight back against corrupt politicians and the bullies of the world." The small crowd in front was clapping and cheering as she spoke. "But more than anything, we're here because three brave middle-school students—Shawn Tucker, Rita Gonzalez, and Sydney Talcott—have brought us all together and led that fight. This one is for them!"

The crowd cheered loudly as the band ripped into the song. The song was amazing. Betty sounded even better live than she did on the album.

Dani and I danced behind the soundboard, singing along. We kept dancing for the rest of the set, singing when we knew the words.

Before their last song, Ben stepped up to the microphone. "Thanks for coming out tonight for this great cause. Thanks to Shawn, Rita, and Sydney for putting this together and inviting us. We're super excited to be sharing the stage with the Tucker Trio and Lite Brite. And at the risk of stepping on the Tucker Trio's toes, we'd like to play one more song that most of y'all hopefully know."

He counted off the beat and then the band blasted into a fantastic song that sounded vaguely familiar. It took me a few moments to recognize what they were playing. Holy crudola. It was "Shady Grove."

I danced my way up front to stand next to Shawn, who looked over at me with a huge grin on his face. As soon as the song ended he turned to me, "Ohmygod, that was amazing! I've never heard 'Shady Grove' so fast or so loud. I love it!"

Just then the lights came up. Shawn and I realized that we were standing in the middle of a big crowd. A huge crowd. Where had all the people come from?

We looked around, slightly stunned. There were at least a hundred people in the room. Maybe more. And all of them were smiling and clapping for the Ward Cleavers.

"Holy crudola," I whispered.

Rita excitedly pushed her way toward us. "Sophia says she just sold the 150th ticket!"

The three of us jumped up and down, squealing.

With a huge sense of relief, I went back to the soundboard to tell Dani the news. But Ben had returned to his spot, and he was busy helping the Tucker Trio get their levels right for their instruments.

I looked around and saw Dani, Betty, and Joey standing at the side of the room. They were laughing and looking like best friends.

I felt a slight pang of jealousy. But I wasn't sure what I was more jealous about, that Dani was hanging out with my friend Betty, or that Betty was hanging out with my friend Dani, or that Joey was hanging out with my two new friends. But it made sense that they'd be hanging out together. They were all older than me and had a lot more in common with each other than they had with me.

Betty looked up, saw me, and waved me over. "Are you ears burnin'?" she said when I got to them.

"What?"

Dani laughed. "We were just convening the first official meeting of the Sydney Talcott Admiration Society."

Joey interjected, "I told them that since I've been a life-long member, I should be the president."

Betty rolled her eyes. "Typical patriarchy power play!" They all laughed.

"Actually, Betty and I had just agreed to arm-wrestle to see which one of us gets to be the president," Dani said.

I just stood there blushing.

And then the lights went dim as the Tucker Trio began to play.

They were unbelievable. I have never heard music played like that before. They played as if they had sold their souls to the devil, but they sang like angels. The vocal harmonies about brought me to tears. If they were rusty from years of retirement, you couldn't tell. They played their instruments with the skill of professionals at the peak of their careers. You could tell how happy the crowd was to be witnessing them playing live. People had their arms around each other, huge grins on their faces, cheering loudly at the end of each song.

It felt like history was being made right there in that ware-house.

At the end of their set, the crowd just kept cheering and calling for more. The front man, who had introduced him-self as Jed Tucker, asked if it was okay to play one more song. The crowd shouted its approval, and I saw Ben gave him the thumbs-up from the back of the room.

"Well, if that's the case, we'd like to invite a few of our newest friends to join us." He then asked Betty and Mr. Snead to join them onstage. Betty walked on with her fiddle and Mr. Snead with his banjo. They both looked like they were going to explode with pride to be sharing the stage with the Tucker Trio. Jed said a few words to the group and then they launched into a stunning version of "Amazing Grace."

I'm pretty sure I was crying from the beauty of it all. Dani had her arm around me, and she was definitely crying too.

When the lights came back on, the crowd had gotten even larger. Much larger. The place was absolutely packed. In the middle of the room, I could see Shawn standing amidst a crowd of his relatives. Next to him was a middle-age white man. I did a double take, thinking that Bradley Winter was standing there. What the heck was he doing here? Then I realized that it must have been Buster Winter, who was laughing and joking around with his in-laws. Even though he was several yards away, it was easy to see that he exuded warmth and compassion. He seemed to be the anti-Bradley Winter.

Shawn caught my eye, pointed to Buster, and waved me over. I had to meet this guy. But as I weaved my way through the crowd, I heard someone call my name. I glanced around, but I didn't see anyone I recognized. It was pretty loud with all the talking, so maybe I imagined it.

"I said, Hello Sydney."

I realized that a young woman with long brown hair and an Against Me T-shirt was speaking to me. I looked at her again.

"Oh my gosh, Ms. Yancey!" I hadn't recognized her with her hair down and out of her professional librarian clothes. "What are you doing here?"

She smiled. "I'm here for the show, of course." She gestured to the crowd around us. "Look at all these people. You've done a great job putting this together, Sydney."

My feeling of pride was quickly squelched when I remembered that all of this had contributed to Ms. Yancey losing her job. She'd been fired because of the campaign against the asphalt plant. Because of me.

"Um, Ms. Yancey," I stammered. "I'm really sorry that you were fired. I know it was my fault…"

Ms. Yancey reached out and put her hand on my shoulder.

She leaned forward and waited until I made direct eye contact with her. "Listen to me, Sydney. It wasn't your fault. I knew the risks I was taking, and I'd gladly take them again. There's a lot going on in that middle school that you don't know about." She paused, like she always seemed to do, before going on. "That you don't need to know about."

"But you lost your job!" I pointed out, feeling guilty.

Ms. Yancey let go of my shoulder and shrugged. "Hey, it just wasn't meant to be. But I've managed to get a job in Franklin with the public library there. It's good. Of course, it's not as much fun without you, Shawn, and Rita hanging around every day."

She gave me a smile and punched me lightly on my shoulder. Then she glanced around. "When's Lite Brite going to start? And how on earth did you get them to come to Beaver Dam? They're one of my favorite bands."

I was dumbstruck. Could Ms. Yancey possibly be any cooler?

But before I could answer, Rita grabbed my arm.

"Sydney, we have a problem. The cops are here."

We pushed our way to the front entrance, where Everett was standing with four uniformed police officers. They had been deep in conversation, but Everett turned to me when I walked up.

"Well, missy. It looks like we got ourselves a couple of problems. The officers here were just sayin' that they've been receivin' noise complaints all evening."

"That's right," said one of the cops, who was taller than the rest, which I guess made him in charge. "We have to respond after receiving two complaints. And we're s'posed to shut things down after the third."

"Uh, how many complaints have you received?" I asked in a small voice.

He looked down at the little notepad he had in his hand.

"Lemme see." He took his time counting. "Twelve. No, wait. Thirteen. Thirteen complaints."

Holy crudola. They were gonna shut us down. Probably even arrest me.

"Funny thing is," he said, scratching his chin, "they're all from the same phone number. And it just so happens we're quite familiar with that particular number. That'd be Mr. Bradley Winter's home number."

"What?"

"Sylvia, our phone operator, tells me that it sounds like the same two people usin' different voices each time."

The officer looked over at Everett. "Darnedest thing is that their house is a good five, six miles from here." The officer glanced at the other police officers standing behind them. "My boys got here half an hour ago and reported that the sound was loud, but probably not too loud." His hardened face broke into a smile. "Fortunately, they also told me the Tucker Trio were just about to start playing, so I only missed a little bit of their set before I could get over here and check things out for myself."

I was confused. "So, we're not getting shut down?"

"Not by me." The office smirked.

"And not by me," came a deep voice behind me.

I turned around to see the fire marshal that Everett had been talking with earlier in the week.

"However," the marshal continued, "I've just done a rough head count and I'd say that you're probably well above the capacity for this space. So do me a favor and don't let any more people in. Can you do that?"

I nodded vigorously.

"Normally, we might have a problem," he glanced around the crowd, "but since I believe almost all of the volunteer fire department is in this room right now, I think we'll be okay."

Everett turned back to the police officer. "Billy, ain't it

against the law to be callin' in and makin' false complaints to the police?"

The officer shot Everett a look. "Don't push your luck, Everett."

"Just makin' an observation."

Everett winked and gave me one of his award-winning smiles.

The set by Lite Brite was amazing. They were definitely peppier and punkier than the Tucker Trio had been, but the crowd loved them to bits.

They were better than I could ever have imagined. I weaved my way to the front of the stage, next to Shawn and Rita, and we watched enthralled. At one point I nudged them both and pointed to Ms. Yancey, who was dancing just to the right of us. I laughed when they both turned back to me with their eyes wide and mouths open.

The band was having so much fun, laughing and dancing as they played. Dani's voice sounded fantastic. The songs from the new album were great, but I preferred the older songs that I could sing along to. Rita surprised me by singing along with a number of the songs as well.

Dani introduced one of their last songs by saying that she had been inspired to write it by our struggle against the asphalt plant. It had a crazy catchy chorus, and at the end, all of the instruments dropped out as Dani got the crowd to join her in singing the chorus over and over again:

Don't trash our future
Don't pave our past.
We've got one world.
We've gotta make it last.

Holy crudola! Lite Brite had written a song inspired by us! I was bursting with joy. But the best was still to come.

Dani dedicated the last song to Rita and me, and invited us to join her onstage. Then the band launched into "The

Unbearable Lightness of Being a Girl." Rita and I leaned into the microphone when it was time to sing the chorus.

The crowd was going crazy with everyone dancing and singing along. And right at the front of the stage, singing loudest, were Mom, Joey and Mr. Snead. I hadn't seen my mom look happy in so long, I almost didn't realize it was her.

Franklin Herald, page A1

Sunday, May 23

"Tucker Trio's Triumphant Return"

Local musical legends the Tucker Trio performed for the first time in over a decade in Beaver Dam this past Friday night. Playing to a sold-out crowd, the Tucker Trio joined three other bands for an impressive night of music and activism. The Trio were joined by local newcomers Bluegrass Lawnmower, Franklin's own punk stalwarts the Ward Cleavers, and pop-punk sensations Lite Brite from Chicago, IL. For the four hundred fans who braved the torrential rains, including this reporter, it was a night to remember.

The concert was held in the warehouse of Everett Campbell's General Hardware Store and was a benefit for a campaign seeking to ban the construction of asphalt plants in Beaver Dam. Mr. Campbell stated that he had loaned out his warehouse, and that the entire concert and campaign was organized by concerned students at Beaver Dam Middle School. Mr. Campbell declined to provide contact information for those students, but supplied the *Franklin Herald* with a copy of a handmade publication that contained a plethora of information about HD Dunkirk Industries, the company seeking to build an asphalt plant on Laurel Ridge Road in Beaver Dam. The land for the proposed plant is currently owned by Bradley S. Winter. Mr. Winter declined to comment for this article, as did his brother, Stephen Winter of the Beaver Dam County Commission. However, investigative reporting by the Franklin Herald has uncovered a long history of questionable business dealings between the

Winter family and HD Dunkirk Industries. Monday's *Franklin Herald* will contain the first article in a five-part report on those connections. [continued on page A2]

16

S o that's how three middle-school students—a proud Affrilachian nerd, his fearless Guatemalan immigrant friend, and the punk rock transplant from Rochester—stopped the asphalt plant from being built.

The concert was a huge success. The newspaper reported that it was sold out with 400 people, but the truth was that we sold almost 450 tickets. I still can't believe they all fit into Everett's warehouse. All the bands refused to take any money, so that gave us enough money to purchase several advertisements in the local paper and a number of radio spots.

We ended up with well over a thousand signatures on the petition, landing the referendum on the June ballot. The county commission tried to fight it, but backed off when the newspaper in Franklin finished their week-long report on HD Dunkirk Industries and its ties to the Winter family.

The first newspaper article drew heavily from our zine. But then the newspaper started reporting on all sorts of questionable behavior by the company, as well as their long-standing business connections with Old Man Winter and his sons.

At first I was amazed at how quickly the newspaper had gotten all of that information. Then Shawn told me that his uncle Buster had come to Beaver Dam the week before the concert and secretly met with reporters from the *Franklin Herald* to expose the Winter family's sordid past. Shawn said that no one knew this was going on until afterwards. It seemed one of the Tucker Trio had called Buster to let him know of their plans to come out of retirement. When Buster heard the reason for the concert, he decided to contact the newspaper.

After the newspaper's coverage, Stephen Winter was forced to resign from the county commission. Granny says she heard a rumor at Harris Teeter that the state has opened an official investigation and would be filing charges against the Winter family and HD Dunkirk Industries.

After the articles were published, the county stopped putting the orange flags in our backyard. We never received any formal explanation, but a friend of Grandpop's who worked for the county told him that the proposed bypass had been "permanently shelved."

In June, the referendum passed by a 3-2 margin. It was the same week that Rita's dad finished his cancer treatment, so we had a lot to celebrate.

For the rest of the school year, Bethany continued to torment me when she could, but I didn't care. The tide had turned at Beaver Dam Middle School. Lots of kids were wearing the Gas Mask Girl T-shirt, and teachers seemed more willing to call Bethany out on her bad behavior.

And her posse seemed to have shrunk by one. One of the twins started keeping her distance from the others. A few weeks before school ended, she showed up with a purple streak in her blond hair, wearing a Ward Cleavers T-shirt.

I'll admit it, she looked pretty cool.

Rita, Shawn, and I have agreed to form a band during summer vacation. Rita said she'd be willing to play drums, and it turns out that she has an amazing singing voice. After seeing the Ward Cleavers, Shawn was excited about all the new ways he could rock out on the fiddle. I still can't play an instrument to save my life, but Betty promised to give me bass lessons. I think I'm finally ready to try to learn again. I know it would make Dad proud of me.

And on the last day of school, I accomplished the once unimaginable: I got a B+ in Mr. Snead's English class.

He was handing back our final papers of the year. When he got to mine, he called out my name: "Talcott, Sydney V."

Looking down at me as he handed me another A paper, he asked, "What does the V stand for, anyway? Victoria? Violet?"

"No. Vicious. Vicious is my middle name."

He looked at me and grinned. "That makes sense, but I would have pegged you as more of a Joan Jett type."

ACKNOWLEDGEMENTS

This book would not have happened without my daughters, Strummer and Barrow, who were both major inspirations, motivators, and critical readers of the manuscript. I am extremely grateful to Cama Duke, Michael Fournier, Todd Taylor, and Jennifer Whiteford for reading earlier drafts of the manuscript. This book is much improved due to their thoughtful engagement, critical insights and generous spirits. I am extremely grateful to the punk MG/YA writers who have come before me, particularly Cecilia C. Pérez, Frank Portman, and Jennifer Whiteford. Thanks to all the Razorcake familia, especially Sean Carswell, Mike Faloon, Kayla Greet, Daryl Gussin, and Donna Ramone. I've also benefited from thoughtful engagement, inspiration, advice and support from Chuck Crews, Melanie Conroy-Goldman, Kevin Freeman, Liz Prince, Doug Reilly, and Nick Ruth. Much respect to Susie Winters, David Sengel, Fog Likely Farm and Watauga Watch for their real-life activism that informed this book. As always, Anna Creadick is a constant source of love, support, and critical pushback. Thanks to Jaynie Royal and all the wonderful people at Fitzroy Books/Regal House Publishing. Special thanks to Amanda Kirk for her friendship and fantastic illustrations. Finally, much gratitude to the incomparable Danny Bailey. Any similarities between the real Danny and the fictional Dani are entirely intentional.